"I'm alway[...]
with Trisha [...]
Brian said.

"Why? Wh[...]
asked, annoyed.

"Nothing," he said quickly. "Don't get so defensive! They're a lot of fun. It's just that you seem, well, quieter, more thoughtful, than the rest of them."

"We don't have a lot in common," Julie admitted, "but I really like them, especially Trisha. She gets me to try things I probably wouldn't do on my own."

"Like go out for the *Gazette*?" Brian asked with a grin.

"Exactly."

"Well, I'm glad you did." He squeezed her fingers. "If you hadn't, I might never have gotten to know you."

Julie felt a warm glow spreading through her. Brian made her feel so special! *But we don't know each other very well*, she reminded herself. She'd better not let her daydreams get out of hand. . . .

Bantam titles in the Sweet Dreams series. Ask your bookseller for titles you have missed:

THE NEWS
IS LOVE

Lauren M. Phelps

BANTAM BOOKS
NEW YORK • TORONTO • LONDON • SYDNEY • AUCKLAND

THE NEWS IS LOVE
A BANTAM BOOK 0 553 29459 8

First publication in Great Britain

PRINTING HISTORY
Bantam edition published 1993

Bantam Books are published by Transworld Publishers Ltd., 61–63 Uxbridge Road, Ealing, London W5 5SA, in Australia by Transworld Publishers (Australia) Pty. Ltd., 15–25 Helles Avenue, Moorebank, NSW 2170, and in New Zealand by Transworld Publishers (N.Z.) Ltd., 3 William Pickering Drive, Albany, Auckland.

Printed and bound in Great Britain by Cox & Wyman Ltd., Reading, Berks.

Chapter One

"Hurry up, Julie!" Trisha Jones tugged at her friend's hand. "We can check on the way to geometry and see if we made it, if you'll stop stalling."

"What's the rush? The activity list will be there all day," Julie Davis said. She wasn't sure she wanted to know whether she'd been chosen for the newspaper staff. Of course, Trisha wasn't really worried about checking the board since she always made the cheerleading squad. Julie, on the other hand, had never tried out for anything at school before, and she was nervous about the result. Still, she had to find out sooner or later.

"Oh, all right." She allowed her bouncy blond friend to pull her down the hallway.

A big crowd had gathered in front of the main bulletin board. Trisha pushed her way to the front, towing Julie with her.

"Aiee!" Trisha squealed, after reviewing the cheerleading squad list. "I made it!"

Julie didn't pay any attention to her, because her eyes were glued to the newspaper staff list. Brian Frederickson, Editor. Lisa Anderson . . . Robert Foster . . . There it was! Julie Davis! She didn't bother to read the rest of the list.

"Well?" Trisha demanded.

"I made it!" To her dismay, Julie's voice came out high and squeaky.

"See? I told you so!" Trisha threw her arms around Julie. "You'd probably have done fine even if you'd tried out for something really exciting."

"Like pep squad, you mean?"

Trisha had done her best to persuade Julie to go out for cheerleading or pep squad, but Julie had flatly refused. In fact, she wasn't too thrilled about signing up for any of the competitive after-school activities. But if she had to pick one, she'd been determined to try something that at least interested her.

The whole thing had been Trisha's idea since she seemed to think that Julie needed to become more involved in school activities. None of this would be happening if her best friend's family hadn't moved away. Julie and

Mary wrote to each other often, but Davenport, Iowa, where Julie lived, was a long way from Seattle, Washington. More than half a continent separated Julie from the girl who had been her best friend since eighth grade, and sometimes she missed Mary desperately.

Julie had been flattered when Trisha, a popular Memorial High cheerleader, had stopped her in the hall shortly after Mary had moved. "The gang is going to Dairy Queen after school," she'd said. "Why don't you come?"

Julie had never quite figured out why Trisha had invited her along that day, but whatever the reason, she was glad. Julie soon discovered that Trisha wasn't the vain snob she'd expected, and they had become good friends. But when Trisha insisted that she go out for an after-school activity, at first it had really irritated Julie.

"How are you ever going to meet any new guys if you don't?" Trisha had asked, as if that settled it.

Trisha ignored Julie's protests that she didn't even want to meet guys. Finally, she'd signed up for the school paper just to shut Trisha up. Now she was glad she'd let Trisha badger her into it. Her journalism class *had* been fun, and she'd often daydreamed about being a reporter for the school paper, but actually doing anything about it had seemed too intimidating.

"Sheri made the squad again, and so did Melanie, but Laura got Janet's spot," Trisha gushed as they edged through the crowd toward their lockers.

"Who's head cheerleader?" Julie dug out her geometry book and slammed the locker shut.

"Melanie, but she's a senior. Next year it'll be me, I just know it. Who else is on the paper?" Trisha asked.

"Brian Frederickson is the editor, and—"

"Brian!" Trisha interrupted. "He's *so* gorgeous! He was in my drama class last year."

"Do you want to hear this or not?" Julie asked, frowning.

"Sorry. Go ahead."

"Lisa Anderson and Robbie Foster and some others. I didn't have time to read the whole list." Julie was too excited to stay mad. She knew Trisha had her best interests at heart.

"Robbie's nice, in a quiet sort of way, but Brian's a real catch. He's not rich or anything, but he's so good-looking," Trisha babbled on. "And he's even nicer than Robbie. I'd go after him if I were you."

"What are you talking about, Trisha? I told you I wanted to work on the paper, not find a boyfriend," Julie said adamantly.

"Well, it never hurts to keep an open mind," Trisha answered, grinning mischievously.

The bell rang as they walked into geometry. Julie made a face and mouthed silently,

"Trisha, you're impossible!" as she slipped into her seat.

But she couldn't just forget Trisha's words. While Mr. Harrison droned on endlessly about the Pythagorean theorem, Julie tried to remember what Brian Frederickson looked like but it was a waste of time. Though his name was vaguely familiar, she couldn't match it with a face.

Finally, she gave up and settled into a pleasant daydream about a masculine voice praising her impressive news story. Gorgeous or not, that was absolutely all she wanted from Brian Frederickson.

"Each of you should be proud that you were chosen for the staff of the *Memorial Gazette*," Ms. Miller, the journalism teacher commended the group gathered in her classroom later that afternoon. "We had nearly twice as many applicants as we needed this year."

Julie had slipped into the room right after the last bell rang and snagged a seat near the front. She couldn't see all of the kids from where she sat, but she'd checked them out pretty carefully as they filed in. At last count, there had been fifteen, including herself. Julie recognized most of the others as juniors and seniors, but a couple looked like freshmen or sophomores. They would be class news reporters, she guessed. About half of those who had showed up were boys, and Julie couldn't help but notice that several of the guys were awfully cute.

"We'll get started as soon as our editor arrives," Ms. Miller continued. "In the meantime I'll—"

She stopped in midsentence as the door burst open.

"Sorry I'm late." But the grin on the latecomer's handsome face said he really wasn't sorry. He strode to the front of the room and dropped into the empty chair beside Julie, flashing her a dazzling smile.

Julie bristled slightly at the boy's casual attitude. This must be Brian Frederickson. If today's performance was his usual style, she wanted absolutely nothing to do with him.

Still, she couldn't resist studying him out of the corner of her eye. Trisha had been right—Brian was gorgeous, with wavy blond hair and big gray-green eyes. Of course, his radiant smile would immediately turn any girl's brain to jelly. But Julie was still confident—not hers!

Ms. Miller gave Brian a hard stare. She didn't seem to like his attitude or his late entrance, either. "Do you have the lists?" she asked.

"The office just finished copying them. That's why I was late," he explained. He reached out to hand them to Ms. Miller, but she waved him away, smiling now. His explanation satisfied her. *At least he hadn't been fooling around in the hallway, talking to some girl, while they waited,* Julie thought.

"We'll pass them out in a minute, Brian." Her eyes skimmed the group again. "In the past, we've tried to let people pick their own assignments. This year, however, since we had such excellent candidates, and so many of the former staff members have graduated, I decided to try something different.

"Each of you was selected because of a special skill or ability, something that will make you an important part of the team. Most of you will find that you've been assigned to the job you wanted. However, some of you may be surprised, maybe even disappointed, with your assignments."

Julie nibbled at her lower lip nervously. Just what did that mean? That they had to do whatever Ms. Miller said, whether they liked it or not? That didn't sound too promising. And what special skill or ability did she have? She thought about some of the comments Ms. Miller had written on her papers last year—that she expressed her feelings well, or that her writing showed compassion and caring. That was fine, but Julie couldn't see the connection to newspaper reporting. *Just what kind of position does expressing my feelings well qualify me for?* Julie wondered.

"Brian and I went over your applications carefully and tried to match your individual talents to the available jobs. I think you'll like what you're doing once you get started. If you're not happy, please just be patient, and remember there's always next year. Those of you who sign up for a second year will definitely have first choice at assignments then."

Julie fidgeted in her chair, growing more worried by the minute, as Ms. Miller motioned to Brian. She wondered what working with him—or rather, *for* him—would be like.

"Brian was chosen as the editor because of his excellent work on the paper last year. I hope you'll all try to make the change from reporter to editor an easy one for him. He'll read through the list of assignments, then pass out copies to everyone." Ms. Miller nodded to Brian and stepped back.

He walked to the front of the room and laid his stack of papers on the table. "First, I'll read the names of the production staff."

Julie listened carefully as he read the names. She knew nothing about printing a paper, and had no desire to learn. If he called her name, she decided she'd just forget the whole thing. It seemed like hours before he finished reading the list, but Julie felt relieved her name hadn't been called.

"Now the news staff." *Brian has a nice voice,* Julie thought, *deep and resonant.* She sat up straighter, concentrating on the names and positions.

"Robbie Foster, sports. Kim Quinn, freshman news. Sarah McLean, sophomore news. Tim Black, junior news." He paused, and Julie felt disappointed. Junior news would have been a good assignment.

"Fred Curtis, senior news. Lisa Anderson, administration news."

Julie's heart dropped to her toes. What was she going to be stuck with? There couldn't be anything good left.

"Julie Davis, opinion columnist . . ."

Opinion columnist? Julie missed the last few assignments as she leaned back against her chair in shock. She wanted to report news, not write opinions! The opinion column in the *Gazette* had always been a bad joke, something no one even bothered to read. This wasn't at all what she'd expected!

She numbly accepted the sheet Brian handed to her and stuffed it into her binder without a second glance. He was still talking, but Julie was too disappointed to pay attention to his words. She did jot down the next meeting date, but she wasn't at all sure she'd be there. Could she live with the stupid assignment she'd been given, even with the promise of first choice next year? When the meeting finally came to an end Julie just wanted to get out of there.

"Julie!" Brian's voice halted her as she started to walk out of the room.

"Yes?" She turned slowly to face him, sure he was able to sense her disappointment.

"Welcome to the team!" He stuck out his hand with a big smile.

"Thank you." She shook his hand, noticing that his grip was firm, his hand big and warm, his smile genuinely friendly.

"Leaving so soon?" Brian asked as she headed for the door. His gray-green eyes sparkled with interest,

"I have to go right home—I didn't even know about the meeting until this morning." Hoping she wasn't blushing, Julie returned his smile tentatively.

"Well, I guess I'll see you at the next meeting then."

With a quick nod, Julie slipped out of the room.

As soon as she was free, she wished she hadn't bolted. There was nothing pressing she had to do at home, and her mother wouldn't be home from work at the Social Services Center for another hour.

Brian's unexpected friendliness had really thrown her, especially after what had just happened with her assignment. If she hadn't gotten out of there, she might have burst into tears or something stupid like that.

As she walked up the hill to her house, she

tried to figure out her feelings about her assignment, and about Brian. Being opinion columnist wasn't what she wanted, but at least she'd be writing. Maybe it would even help her find the confidence to show her poetry to someone one day.

As for Brian, she wondered which was the *real* Brian—the wise guy who had walked in late, or the polite young man who had welcomed her so warmly. By the time she let herself in the door, Julie was hopelessly confused.

Chapter Two

"I am *so* tired. Every muscle in my body aches," Trisha announced dramatically the next afternoon, dropping onto the orange plastic bench with a groan. "I'd forgotten how much work cheerleading is."

"What did you expect?" Julie asked. "All that exercise is bound to hurt at first." She fanned her face to cool off from the walk after school to Dairy Queen. The heat of Indian summer had been a shock after the relatively cool classroom.

Trisha picked up the old-fashioned phone at their table and ordered a strawberry soda for herself and a diet cola for Julie.

"How did your first newspaper meeting go yesterday?" she asked.

Julie shrugged. "Not too terrific."

Trisha leaned forward, looking concerned. "Why? What went wrong?"

"It just wasn't what I expected, that's all," Julie said, sighing. "I didn't get the job I wanted. I'm not a reporter."

"Don't keep me in suspense. What's your assignment?" Trisha asked as a waitress delivered their orders.

"The opinion columnist. I'm supposed to write the opinion column!" To Julie's frustration, Trisha burst into laughter. "What's so funny?"

"*You* are! I thought you were going to say you were in charge of delivering the papers or something," Trisha said between giggles.

"I might as well be." Refusing to respond to Trisha's good-natured teasing, Julie turned away.

"So what's wrong with writing the opinion column?" Trisha asked, swallowing her laughter.

"It's not news, and you know it's the world's biggest joke. Nobody takes it seriously. Besides, I don't have any opinions worth printing."

"That's not true," Trisha protested. "You have lots of good ideas, Julie. Besides, they don't all have to be *your* opinions. You can do surveys, or have people write in, things like that." Trisha spooned up a bit of vanilla ice

13

cream from her soda glass. "Mmm—delicious!"

Julie watched enviously. Maybe she should have gone out for pep squad after all. If she were getting as much exercise as Trisha was, she could be eating ice cream instead of sipping diet soda. And she wouldn't be worrying about the stupid newspaper.

"Trisha, no one even *reads* the opinion column. It's so bad that people just skip it."

"But Julie," Trisha said, "that's exactly the point. It's what makes this such a perfect opportunity!"

"For what? What are you talking about?" Hadn't Trisha been listening to her? The opinion column was a disaster.

"It's obvious. *Why* don't people read it?"

"Because it's so bad," Julie repeated, irritated.

"Right!" Trisha slapped the table excitedly. "So all *you* have to do is write an interesting column, and everyone will want to read it."

"I don't know . . ." Julie didn't think she could write an opinion column at all, much less an interesting one.

"Just think about it. You'll make a name for yourself as the one who turned the column around. You can have an impact on what happens at school, too!"

"How could I do that?" Trisha's reasoning was beginning to sound interesting, but Julie wasn't sure what her friend had in mind. Or was Trisha still just trying to cheer her up?

"Well . . ." Trisha stared off into space, then turned to Julie, wide-eyed. "For instance, what if you interviewed Mr. Higgins, the cook, and discovered he was putting some kind of weird chemicals in the food? You could write a column expressing your opinion about it. I read about some kids who did that and got the cafeteria to change the kind of food it served."

Julie was beginning to see the endless possibilities. "You mean, kind of like investigative reporting? I never thought of it that way. Maybe I could check with students at Washington High and Barnes and see if their dress code is the same as ours. If they're different, I could find out why. That might make an interesting column. . . ."

"Sure! There are tons of things you can do."

Before they could explore any more ideas, their friends Sheri and Laura arrived. Julie chatted with the other girls as she finished her drink, but her mind kept wandering. Suddenly she was brimming with ideas for her column and it was hard to pay attention to the latest gossip.

Forgetting her earlier misgivings, Julie could hardly wait for the next newspaper meeting.

On Monday morning, Allan Davis pushed his glasses up on his narrow nose, and smiled at his daughter. "Don't you look nice today. Makeup and everything. Is there a special occasion?"

Julie blushed as she sat down and sprinkled a little sugar on her cornflakes. Trust her father to notice that she had brushed on mascara to accent her large, brown eyes, put on some lipstick for a change, and taken extra care blow-drying her, brown hair.

"You finally decided to wear your new pink sweater, too," Carol Davis noted with a smile. "I was beginning to think you didn't like it."

"I was saving it for something special," Julie admitted.

"What makes today special?" her father asked.

"Well, I told you that I'm the new opinion columnist for the *Memorial Gazette*. Today I get my first story."

"That's great," Mr. Davis exclaimed. "I loved working on the paper when I was in college. I remember writing a scathing editorial about cheating on exams that shook up the whole school!"

"That's what I want to do," Julie said eagerly. "Write about something that will stir up some excitement."

"I'm sure you'll do a great job, honey." Her father sipped his coffee and leaned back in his chair. "You know, for a while I thought I might

16

take up journalism as a career. Who would have thought I'd end up selling appliances?"

Julie's mother stood at the sink, slicing vegetables and dropping them into the slow cooker so dinner would be ready when they all got home.

"What do you think, Mom?" Julie asked.

"I'm happy for you, dear . . ." she said hesitantly.

"You don't sound very happy," Julie pointed out.

"Of course I am. It's just . . ." Mrs. Davis turned around to face her. "Are you sure you're ready for this, Julie?"

"Of course I am," Julie replied, surprised. "I even have the subject for my first column. It took me ages to pick it out."

Her mother spoke slowly, choosing her words carefully. "Honey, I know how sensitive you are. I'm just afraid you'll end up getting your feelings hurt. For instance, how will you feel if someone doesn't like your story?"

"I can take it," Julie said, but her mother's words startled her. She hadn't even considered that possibility.

"Are you sure? I'm sure you write beautiful poetry, but you won't ever let anyone read it because you can't stand the idea of criticism," Mrs. Davis said gently.

"That's different," Julie protested.

"Don't discourage her, Carol," her father said. "This will be a good experience."

"I suppose you're right, Allan," her mother said with a sigh, "but I can't help worrying."

Mr. Davis looked directly at his daughter, his eyes serious, "Working on the newspaper, you're bound to have plenty of new experiences, Julie, and not all of them will be pleasant. Some people will disagree with what you write, and that could make you angry, or hurt your feelings. But just because something is hard or scary is no reason not to do it."

Julie gave her father a kiss, then hugged her mother. "Don't worry, Mom. I'll be fine," she said confidently.

She hurried out the door. As soon as she got outside she dismissed her mother's concern. There was a newspaper meeting during study hall, and with a little luck, she might be able to get started on her first story after school.

Although some of Julie's excitement had worn off after her talk with Trisha, coming up with ideas for her column over the weekend had been fun. Maybe the job wouldn't be too bad. Anyway, she'd signed up for it, and she certainly was no quitter.

She was looking forward to seeing Brian again, too. She knew it was silly, but she'd spent a lot of time thinking about him over the past two days. Though the way he had walked in late to the meeting had irritated her, he'd had a good explanation, he *was* cute, and he had been so nice to her. . . .

Julie fidgeted through her morning classes, and jumped out of her seat when it was time for study hall. She couldn't believe it when her locker door stuck. By the time she managed to get it open and stow her books, instead of being early for the meeting, she was late.

Julie saw that Ms. Miller had moved the chairs in her classroom into a circle, so she couldn't even sneak in and quietly take a seat in the back. She was standing outside the door, wondering what to do, when Brian rushed over to her.

"Julie! Don't tell me you're late, too." He grinned at her.

"My locker stuck." Julie's cheeks heated at her dumb response, but Brian didn't seem to notice.

"I don't have such a good excuse. I just stopped to talk to Brad about our plans for the canned food drive, and I lost track of time. C'mon. We better go." Taking her hand, Brian led her to a pair of empty chairs.

"This will be a short meeting," Ms. Miller was saying as they sat down. "I just want to be sure you all know what to do." She went on to tell them that the deadline for the next issue of the *Gazette* was Friday, then handed out a list of instructions. Most of the rules had to do with common errors in spelling and

19

grammar they should make sure to avoid. "Since most of you haven't done this before, you'll need to clear your topics with Brian or me before you start. Please plan to meet with one of us as soon as possible, so you can make the deadline."

Julie frowned. She had to get permission before she started writing. This was worse than English class!

The meeting broke up soon after that. She was walking out of the room, mulling over what Ms. Miller had said, when Brian caught up with her.

"Julie, wait. We need to talk."

"About what?" she asked, more sharply than she intended.

"About your column, of course. You heard Ms. Miller—one of us has to okay your topic, and I hereby volunteer." When he smiled like that, Julie noticed the dimple on his left cheek.

"When do you want to talk about it?" she asked, smiling too.

"Now's a good time, if you're not busy. Let's wait until everyone leaves, though."

Why does Brian want to wait until we're alone? Julie wondered. Maybe he wanted to talk about something more personal than the column. Her heart pounded as Ms. Miller and the others left the classroom.

Brian proceeded to sit down beside her and

pull out a notebook. Apparently he really *did* want to talk about her column.

"Have you come up with any ideas yet?" he asked.

"Oh, yes. I thought about it a lot this weekend," Julie said eagerly. She was glad she had written her ideas down, because suddenly she was so nervous that she didn't think she'd be able to remember them on her own. She handed him her list, and Brian studied it for a moment.

"It's the wrong season for an article on planting trees," he said, "and only the girls would be interested in a piece on skirt lengths. We don't want to start the year with a column that will only appeal to half the students."

"I suppose you're right," Julie admitted reluctantly.

"A story on stray dogs and the ASPCA sounds interesting, but how does it relate to Memorial High?" He looked up from the list, his eyebrows drawn together.

Julie struggled to find a connection. "Well, lots of students have pets . . ." she began.

Brian shook his head. "Not good enough. This is a *school* newspaper." He studied her list again. "Now, here's one that sounds promising. What kind of piece were you thinking of doing on the school library?"

"Well, I . . ." Julie tried to collect her thoughts, but his abrupt dismissal of her other ideas made her feel so stupid and incompetent that she drew a blank.

"You have to have some kind of focus, Julie." Brian sounded impatient. "For instance, a story on the library budget requires different research than one on whether students have enough study space."

Julie bristled at the irritation in his voice, but she admitted he had a point. Since she hadn't really thought the whole thing through she had to think fast that second. "I thought I'd do a column on . . . on the book selection process."

Brian nodded. "Now there's a good idea, and I don't believe it's ever been done. Most of the kids probably don't even know how the library books are chosen—at least I don't."

"Then the library idea is okay?" Julie asked, to be absolutely sure. She was still insulted by his critique of her other ideas.

"It's terrific." Brian grinned and leaned closer. "And I know you'll do a good job." The way he looked at her made Julie feel like she was the only girl in the world. He was *so* good-looking—and that smile . . .

The rest of the day dragged for Julie because she was so eager to begin her project. Finally, classes were over, and she headed straight for the library, hoping Mr. Riggs, the librarian, wasn't too busy to talk to her.

There were only half a dozen students in

sight. Mr. Riggs sat behind the checkout desk, reading a magazine.

"Mr. Riggs, do you have a few minutes?" Julie asked.

The tall, balding librarian smiled at her. "Why yes, Julie. What can I do for you?"

Julie explained that she was a columnist for the school paper. "And I'd like to do my first column on the library," she added.

"Great." The librarian beamed as he came out from behind the desk, motioning her to sit at one of the empty tables. "Now what exactly would you like to know?"

"I'm interested in book selection," Julie said, opening her notebook and uncapping her pen. "How does a book get into the school library?"

"It's a long process, actually." Mr. Riggs' eyes took on a faraway look as he explained how the library staff read book catalogs, course schedules, and book reviews to come up with a list of potential purchases.

Julie made notes as he talked, pausing to ask questions now and then. *This isn't so different from news reporting, after all*, she thought.

"After my staff has developed a preliminary list, we send it to the library committee for approval," Mr. Riggs continued.

"The library committee?" Julie repeated. "I never even heard of the library committee. Who's on it?"

"Four teachers, four parents, two members of administration, and one school board member."

"No students?"

"No." Mr. Riggs gave her a surprised look, as if he thought that was a silly question.

"Does this committee do the actual choosing, then?" Julie prompted.

"Not exactly—it only has veto power, so it can't add books to the list."

Mr. Riggs glanced up as two girls came over to the desk, their arms full of books. "Duty calls. You'll have to excuse me for a minute, Julie."

"Okay." As she was collecting her thoughts she realized that something wasn't right. The students were the ones who used the library. Why didn't they have anything to say about what books were available to them? There had to be some way they could make their needs known.

Mr. Riggs returned and sat down. "What else would you like to know, Julie?"

"What if a student requests a certain book that the library doesn't have?" she asked.

"We might consider buying it next year, but that only happens rarely. Usually, we select books that fit the classes being offered or that cover issues the teachers think are important. Books are a big investment, you know. They must be chosen very carefully."

And the students who use them aren't important enough to be consulted about what they read? Julie thought, outraged. She pressed her lips together to hold back the angry words in her mind. Maybe she had misunderstood.

"Surely the students have *some* input into the selection process," she pressed.

Mr. Riggs shook his head. "Not really. After all, most kids don't know the first thing about selecting books."

"They know what they like to read," Julie said, her voice rising slightly. "They also have a pretty good idea what information they need to prepare for their classes."

"Maybe so," Mr. Riggs said. He was beginning to sound irritated. "But this is a school library. We must provide the kind of reading material that the school board, the parents, and the teachers feel is most appropriate for the students. Besides, we have a very limited budget, and there's a public library nearby if someone wants a book we don't have."

Julie closed her notebook a little too hard, forcing herself to smile. "I understand. You've been very helpful, Mr. Riggs. Thank you so much for your time."

She quickly walked out of the library feeling excited that she'd hit upon something. The kids at Memorial High didn't have a voice in something as important as choosing books for the library!

She ran into Trisha who was on her way to cheerleading practice. "How did it go?" Trisha asked.

"Great!" Julie said enthusiastically, putting on her coat. "Can't talk now, Trish—I've got a column to write, and it's going to be a zinger!"

Chapter Three

Julie sat at her computer for hours that night. She'd felt a little guilty about saying she would be done soon when her mother peeked into the bedroom to say good night around ten-thirty. But she just had to capture the sense of outrage she'd felt at what she had learned from Mr. Riggs.

Then Julie carefully revised her work. After a whole semester of listening to Ms. Miller emphasize the importance of revision, she could hardly turn in a first draft. As she went over her column, Julie realized that in her haste, she had forgotten to run the spell check, and she had also written some sentence fragments. What would Brian think if she turned in such sloppy work? She didn't turn off the computer until the column was perfect, but she decided to wait until morning to print it out.

As Julie drifted off to sleep, she began to think about Brian. Maybe it was silly to get so excited just because he was friendly to her, but he had such an adorable dimple. . . . She didn't remember her stomach fluttering this way last year with Ron Harrington, and he'd been her boyfriend. Well, *almost* her boyfriend, Julie amended. They had been good friends, and had dated a few times. They had kissed once, but it hadn't been anything special for either one of them. Maybe that was why they had decided to stay just friends.

I'm probably getting carried away, Julie thought. Brian could never be interested in her. Trisha had been right—Brian was gorgeous—and smart, too. With his looks and personality, he could probably date any girl he wanted. Still, the memory of his smile filled Julie with a warm, happy feeling as she finally fell asleep.

The next morning, Julie could hardly force her eyelids open. But the extra effort had been worthwhile. Her first column was ready for Brian two days early. Julie hoped he would be impressed by her promptness. She printed her column out while she dressed for school.

She chose her pretty peach blouse and even

28

wore her best brown wool slacks instead of her usual jeans. When she was finished, she fastened a gold barrette in her hair and looked in the mirror, which reflected a far more sophisticated girl than the usual Julie.

Her father glanced up when she came into the kitchen.

"Makeup again?" he asked, looking surprised. "You're turning into a real young lady." Julie blushed as he took a closer look at her. "You do look tired, though, Julie."

"Aren't you getting enough rest, dear?" Mrs. Davis asked, studying her daughter.

"I just had a little trouble falling asleep last night," Julie said, feeling guilty. It wasn't exactly a lie. It *was* pretty hard to fall asleep sitting at a computer!

By the time she got to school, however, Julie felt much better. Now if she could just find a way to go over her column with Brian in private. . . .

He walked by her locker while she was gathering some books, and Julie impetuously called his name.

"How's it going, Julie?" When Brian smiled at her, she noticed that his blue-green shirt intensified the color of his eyes. "Have you been working on your column?"

"Actually, it's finished," Julie blurted out.

"Hey, you're a real early bird!" He chuckled. "That's great. It's a lot easier for me if I don't get everyone's stuff at the last minute. Want to give it to me now?"

That wasn't what she'd had in mind at all. Julie hoped they'd have time to talk about it, maybe in the library where they would have to sit close together and whisper to keep from disturbing people.

"I thought you'd want to go over it with me," she said. Her words sounded more demanding, pushier, than she'd planned, but it was too late to take them back. "Since it is my first column . . ."

"Good idea. Why don't we meet in Ms. Miller's classroom after school?"

Delighted, Julie beamed at him. "Okay! See you then."

For the rest of the day, Julie felt as if her feet didn't quite touch the ground. When the last bell rang, she hurried to Ms. Miller's room, but Brian wasn't there yet. Julie didn't worry since she had been discovering that he was never on time. Brian was just so busy with his work on the newspaper and the canned food drive. Julie had even seen his name on another sign-up sheet, volunteering to drive senior citizens on errands after school. And he obviously loved to talk. That took time, too.

Brian dashed in just as she took her column out of her book bag.

"Mr. Simonson wouldn't let us pick up our

homework assignments until after the last bell, and then it was a zoo," he explained, dropping into the chair beside her. "Is that your column?"

Suddenly apprehensive, Julie gave it to him. It had seemed perfect last night, but now she wasn't so sure. Maybe she should have read it one more time before handing it in.

"Hold on a minute while I read it," he said smiling.

As he read, his smile began to fade. When Julie was sure he must be finished, he just stared at the paper without speaking. Finally, she couldn't stand the suspense.

"What do you think of it?" she asked timidly.

"Don't you think it's a little one-sided?" Brian questioned.

"One-sided?" Julie repeated, confused. "It's *supposed* to be one-sided. This is the opinion column."

"I know that, Julie," he said, "but the opinions have to be grounded in reality."

"My column *is* grounded in reality." She felt her temper begin to rise, but she tried to control it. Obviously, Brian didn't understand. If she just explained calmly, she was sure everything would be fine. "Mr. Riggs explained the whole book selection procedure to me. Every word of it is true," she said, trying to keep her tone neutral.

"Even this part about . . ." Brian skimmed down through the column. " 'Administrative dictatorship' . . ." He ran a finger down a little farther. " 'Thought control and blatant censorship'?"

"Well, what would *you* call it?" Julie asked indignantly. "We students aren't even consulted by the people who choose the books we read!"

"Okay, so it's not the best procedure in the world," he admitted. "I think you should tone this column down a bit . . ."

"I will not!" Julie exclaimed before she could stop herself. "This isn't a question of bad procedure. You should have seen the look on Mr. Riggs' face when I suggested that students should have a voice in choosing their own books. You'd have thought I wanted to play rock music in the library or something!"

"Come on, Julie, be reasonable." Brian looked exasperated. "The school pays for printing the *Gazette*. We can't go around pointing fingers at people, especially when some of them are members of the school board."

"But in this case it's the truth," she insisted.

"True or not, this column is too strongly worded," Brian told her. "You'll have to revise it."

Julie glared at him. "You mean turn it into the same kind of boring column the paper printed last year? Well, I won't do it!"

"That's your choice, Julie, but I can't print it like this," Brian said calmly.

"Fine. Then we'll just forget the whole thing!" Fighting back her tears, Julie snatched the paper out of his hands and stuffed it into her book bag. She was almost running as she headed for the door.

Before she could escape, Brian called after her, "If you change your mind, the deadline's still Friday."

Luckily, there was no one in the hall as she dashed to her locker. She struggled to get her emotions under control while she took out her jacket and waited for Trisha to finish cheer-leading practice.

Brian's criticism had hurt and made her so angry! The more she thought about it, the angrier she got. She couldn't remember the last time she had been so infuriated. The nerve of him—telling her to rewrite her piece so the school board would like it! Whatever happened to freedom of the press?

She and Trisha sat in a booth at Dairy Queen a while later, and Julie told her friend all about her argument with Brian. She took a long sip of her chocolate ice-cream soda and sighed. Even the special treat wasn't cheering her up.

"So what?" Trisha shrugged. "Telling you what's wrong with your article is the editor's job."

"He thinks *everything* is wrong with it," Julie moaned. "With editors like Brian, it's no wonder no one reads the opinion column!"

"Personally, I think you're overreacting," Trisha said.

Julie scowled. "I bet you wouldn't feel that way if Melanie kept criticizing your cheerleading."

"But she does," Trisha told her. "Today she told me that my splits needed work, my timing was off, and my cartwheels were sloppy."

"So what are you going to do?"

Trisha grinned. "Practice my cartwheels and my splits," she said nonchalantly. She took a sip of her milkshake. "I'm not going to worry about my timing, though. It was Laura who was out of step, not me. She doesn't know what she's doing yet."

"I do, too," Laura said, coming up behind them and slipping into the booth next to Trisha. "Remember, I was on the pep squad at Washington before I transferred here. I just don't have the hang of these new routines yet."

Trisha smiled at her, and waved to Sheri, who had arrived with Laura. Laura sat next to Julie. "Then you admit you were out of step."

"Sure do." Laura grinned back. "But don't expect me to admit it to Melanie. She yells at me enough as it is."

Julie tapped Sheri on the shoulder. "Time to

let me out. Mr. Harrison gave us a ton of homework, and I have a paper to write for my English class."

"Don't work too hard," Laura called after her.

"I won't."

On the way home, Julie walked slowly, thinking about what Trisha had said. Was she overreacting? *No,* she told herself vehemently. There was a big difference between helping someone learn the right way to do a cartwheel and telling them what they could or couldn't write. How did Brian expect her to write an opinion column if he wouldn't let her express an opinion?

If she didn't do what he wanted, her career in journalism would be over before it even began. Her column would never see the light of day, and no one would ever find out about the shocking way library books were chosen. If she rewrote the column, people would know what was happening. Maybe she *could* actually change things. Her classmates might even be upset enough to circulate a petition. In fact, she could even suggest it in her column.

Still, Brian's reaction had really hurt. Julie had thought he was so special, but he wasn't. He was just plain mean! He had such nice eyes, though. Even when she had refused to rewrite the column, he had given her a chance to change her mind. She should have said something then, but what could she have said? That he had hurt her feelings? That she didn't know what he wanted from her? Even if she decided to rewrite the stupid column, she didn't see how she could ever face Brian again, after the way they had argued.

Trisha and her friends seemed to take Melanie's criticism in stride. Could Julie learn to do that with Brian? She struggled to hold back the tears welling up in her eyes.

One thing was sure. Brian Frederickson wasn't worth crying over, and neither was his stupid newspaper!

Chapter Four

"Hey, Julie! Wait up."

Julie turned around as she hurried to biology class and saw that it was Brian calling her. She reluctantly slowed her pace so he could catch up. "What is it? I don't want to be late for class," she said, not returning his smile.

"What do you have next?"

"Biology—Ms. Trent."

"Trent? It takes her forever to get started. She won't notice if you're a little late. Besides, this will only take a minute. What are you doing Saturday?"

She was about to tell him that *some* people thought being late was rude when suddenly his words sank in. He wanted to know what she was doing Saturday. Could that possibly mean he was going to ask her out? No way, not after the way they had argued the day before. She had been up half the night thinking about that stupid column. Now just thinking about Brian's earlier behavior rekindled her anger. He probably wanted to meet with her so he could tell her how to write her next column, and Julie didn't think she could handle that.

"I'm going to be pretty busy," she hedged. "There are a lot of things I have to take care of. . . ."

"I'm taking Harvey to the park. Do you want to come along? I thought we could take a picnic or something."

Julie stared at him, unable to believe her ears. A picnic? He wanted her to go on a *picnic* with him? Julie fought the urge to ask if he was out of his mind. "Who's Harvey?" she asked instead.

"My dog. He's a basset hound. So what do you say? Want to go?"

Julie clutched her books and debated as the first bell rang. She felt so confused. Except for that argument about her column, Brian had been awfully nice to her. And she really *did* like him. By Saturday, she could have rewritten her column and forgotten all about their disagreement. Why not accept his invitation?

She took a deep breath and nodded. "Okay. Can I bring anything?"

"Dessert would be nice," Brian said. He beamed at her, making her heart thump wildly. "I'll pick you up about eleven."

"Great. Well, I'd better get to class," she said, returning his smile shyly.

"See you later, Julie." He turned and walked down the hall, whistling. Julie had taken two steps toward her biology class when a shout stopped her.

"Julie!" Brian sprinted back down the hall. "I forgot to ask where you live."

Grinning, Julie gave him her address, then hurried into her class. Unbelievable! Brian Frederickson had actually asked her out! A picnic might not be a *big* date, but it was definitely a date. She could hardly wait to tell Trisha.

That evening, she rewrote her column, figuring that the sooner she got it out of the way, the sooner she could think about Saturday. It wasn't as difficult as she had expected. First she crossed out everything that Brian had objected to. Then she tried to put most of the ideas back in, but much less belligerently.

When she finished, Julie stretched out on her bed to read the revised column. While all of her important points were still there, she had added several good, solid reasons why students should be allowed to participate in the book selection process.

She hated to admit it, but Brian had been right. The revised article was more persuasive, and it read better than her first attempt.

Julie got up and wandered over to the window, staring out into the night. Who would ever have thought her life would change so drastically in such little time? Just last spring, she had been one of those girls no one noticed. Now she had an important newspaper job, *and* a date with one of Memorial High's most popular boys! What would Mary think if she could see her now?

Thinking of her friend made her feel a twinge of guilt. Since Julie had started working on the *Gazette*, she had neglected her letter writing. She decided to answer Mary's most recent letter right then.

Mary's letters were much more cheerful than the first ones she had written. She was making friends, and she'd joined a nature club to explore the Pacific shoreline. Her second letter mentioned that she'd also joined the school drama club. Julie was surprised by that. It was hard to imagine her quiet friend getting up on a stage. But then, who would have thought she would end up writing an opinion column for the *Memorial Gazette*? Julie smiled and started typing at her computer.

She commented on her friend's new projects, and answered all Mary's questions about mutual friends. By the time she was ready to reveal her own news, she knew just what to say.

I was glad to hear that you're starting to like Seattle, she wrote. *You sounded pretty depressed at first, and so was I. Like you, though, I'm getting used to it.*

Trisha Jones and I have become friends. Of course, she could never replace you, but she's really nice.

Guess what! I'm the new opinion columnist for the Memorial Gazette! Julie told Mary about her first assignment, and how Brian had made her rewrite it.

At first, I was really angry, but I got over it. After all, that's his job. She smiled ruefully. Those words were much easier to write than they were to accept, especially when it was her work being torn to pieces.

Other than that, things are going pretty well. Brian is awfully nice, except for making me do rewrites. Maybe you remember him. He has big, gray-green eyes, blond hair, and a dimple. I think he likes me. We're going on a picnic Saturday.

Julie frowned at the screen. That didn't do justice to the importance of their date, but she didn't want to exaggerate either.

By the time she finished writing, it was too

late to call Trisha and tell her about the picnic. She knew her friend would tease her about how she had said she didn't want a boyfriend. But that was before she met Brian. As she got ready for bed, Julie imagined Trisha's surprise. She was still smiling when she fell asleep.

On Friday, Julie caught Brian between classes and handed him her rewrite. He seemed pleased that she had changed her mind, and reminded her of their date the next day. Julie said she was looking forward to it, and hurried off to class.

That afternoon, she planned to go right home and make the dessert she had promised to bring on the picnic. She ran into Trisha in the hall, and the girls walked home together. Julie was dying to share her big news, but Trisha kept chattering on about the latest gossip around school. They were almost at Trisha's house before she was able to get a word in edgewise.

"By the way," Julie said, trying to sound casual, "I won't be able to go biking tomorrow." Earlier in the week, the girls had talked about bicycling on Saturday along the river, if the weather was good.

"Why not? It would be fun," Trisha said.

"I know, but I'm going on a picnic."

"With your family?" Trisha asked.

42

"No." Julie paused dramatically. "With Brian."

"What?" Trisha exclaimed. "Why didn't you say something earlier? That's great!"

"I didn't want to make a big deal of it," Julie murmured.

"It *is* a big deal. Brian Frederickson!" Trisha sighed. "He's so good-looking. All the girls will be green with envy."

"I wish you wouldn't tell anybody yet," Julie said, suddenly uncomfortable. Who knew what Trisha might say? She wouldn't exactly lie, but Trisha had a tendency to exaggerate.

"Oh, I get it." Trisha nodded. "You want to see how it goes before you say anything. I'll keep your secret, but I'm sure everything will be perfect." She gave Julie a big hug.

As she walked the last few blocks alone, Julie felt happy. When Mary moved away, she had doubted that she would ever find another close friend, but now it seemed that she and Trisha were beginning to form a special bond.

It was after five when Julie finally sat down with her mother's cookbooks. She laid them all out on the kitchen table and opened them to the dessert sections. What would Brian like? She had no idea, and most of the recipes sounded complicated. Julie was so busy reading that she didn't hear her mother's car pull into the driveway.

"What are you doing, honey?" Mrs. Davis asked as she walked into the kitchen.

"Mom, what do boys like for dessert?"

Mrs. Davis laughed. "Boys like anything sweet. Why do you ask?"

"I'm going on a picnic tomorrow, and I'm supposed to bring dessert."

"With a boy?" Her mother looked interested.

"With Brian Frederickson." When Mrs. Davis looked blank, Julie added, "The newspaper editor."

"I thought you didn't like him."

"Oh, no. He's . . ." Julie blushed. How could she describe her feelings about Brian? "We had kind of an argument, but that's all over now. He's involved in all kinds of school projects, he's really nice, and he just happens to be *gorgeous*!" Julie grinned. "He invited me to go on this picnic with him, but I forgot to ask what kind of dessert he likes."

"Chocolate chip cookies are always a good bet," Mrs. Davis suggested.

"They're pretty boring."

"They don't have to be," her mother said. "Why don't I help you? We could add walnuts and bits of white chocolate, then frost them. And you might bring some fresh fruit, too."

Julie thought that sounded great. She was glad her mother had offered to help, because her cooking skills were pretty limited to macaroni and cheese, sandwiches, and salads.

After supper that night, Julie and her mother set to work. Measuring and stirring the thick dough was fun, and Julie stole a few chocolate morsels and walnuts before adding the rest of them to the mixture. "This isn't so difficult," she said to her mother as she slid the first batch into the oven and set the timer. Then they started making the frosting.

"Since you're going out with the editor, I assume your column is going well," Mrs. Davis said.

Julie smiled. "I handed in the rewrite of my first column today," she said, pleased.

"I'm glad I was wrong about your being too sensitive for this job. You really are just like your father—he never lets anything get him down."

Julie concentrated on spooning cookie batter onto the second cookie sheet. She didn't want to worry her mother by telling her how right she had been. Besides, she was sure Brian would never hurt her feelings again.

The next morning, Julie couldn't sit still. The weather report had predicted a beautiful, sunny fall day, but she couldn't help peeking out the window half a dozen times to be sure no clouds were gathering. Sure enough, the sky remained blue, and when she opened her window, the breeze that ruffled her hair was crisp and cool.

Julie tried on half the clothes in her closet before deciding on jeans and a bright yellow sweatshirt. Her denim jacket would be warm enough, she thought as she tied a yellow scarf around her hair, only to take it right off because it seemed too dressy. Her yellow sunburst earrings looked good, though. After putting on just a little makeup, Julie was finally satisfied with her appearance.

Brian arrived fifteen minutes early, looking wonderful in faded jeans, a red turtleneck, and navy blue windbreaker. Suddenly panic-stricken, Julie wondered what someone like Brian could possibly see in her. Yet he seemed glad to be there, and Julie soon relaxed as she introduced him to her parents. Brian and her dad immediately started discussing baseball like old friends while Julie followed her mother to the kitchen to get the cookies and fruit.

By the time they came back, Brian and Mr. Davis were having a friendly argument about the relative merits of the Cubs and the Cardinals. Julie was beginning to wonder if they'd ever stop, when Mrs. Davis cleared her throat and said pointedly, "The kids probably want to get going, Allan."

"Of course." Mr. Davis grinned at his wife. "Brian's a Cards fan. I was just trying to show him the error of his ways." He turned back to Brian. "Maybe one of these days you'll change your mind about the Cubs," he joked.

"Don't count on it. I come from a long line of Cards fans," Brian said with a laugh. "Nice meeting you both." He took Julie's hand, and they hurried out the door.

Brian opened the door to his navy blue sedan for Julie, but the front seat was already occupied by a dog with the biggest, most mournful brown eyes Julie had ever seen. His jowls drooped, and his ears hung nearly to the ground. The strip of white running down his long face only accented his pitiful expression.

Brian frowned. "Into the back, Harvey," he said sternly.

The dog looked pleadingly at Brian, and when that didn't work, he turned his big brown eyes to Julie, melting her heart.

"Now," Brian said, pointing.

Harvey shook his ears and crawled between the bucket seats, his tail drooping.

"You'd better keep the dessert in the front seat," Brian told Julie. "Harvey can't resist sweets."

"Can you?" she asked, smiling.

"Nope. Maybe you should hold on to that bag until after lunch," he said with an answering smile.

When they reached the park, Julie saw a few children playing on the swings at the top of the hill, but the tables down by Duck Creek were all deserted. Brian pulled over to a shady area of oak trees. "How's this?"

"Looks fine to me," Julie said as they got out. "It's really nice here."

Ignoring the picnic tables, Brian spread a red plaid blanket on the ground and set a cooler on one corner while Harvey gingerly climbed out of the backseat. He shook his whole body, then trotted over to Julie and peered up at her, his tail wagging. Seeing his interest, Julie put her bag of cookies and fruit into the cooler for safekeeping.

"You're a real mooch, aren't you?" she asked, bending down to stroke Harvey's head. The dog wagged his tail harder and gave her hand a long, wet lick.

"I think he likes you," Brian said with a smile. "Want to take a walk down by the creek before lunch?"

"Sure. It's early yet," Julie agreed.

"Great. Come on, Harvey." The dog followed reluctantly, howling softly as he slid a little on the rocky embankment leading down to the water. Julie's sneakers weren't made for climbing, and she started to slip, too, but Brian took her hand to steady her. When they were back on level ground, he kept holding her hand, and a warm feeling washed over her.

"By the way," he said, "I read your revised column."

Julie tensed. "What did you think of it?" Was he going to ruin their date by picking it apart?

"It's great," Brian said to her relief. "You got all your points across in a way that won't offend anyone. You're a talented writer, Julie."

"Why, thank you!" Julie glowed with pleasure. "Doing the revision wasn't as hard as I thought it would be," she admitted. "I'm sorry I blew up at you the other day. I know you were just doing your job."

Brian shrugged. "It's something all writers have to learn to put up with. The only thing I don't rewrite about a dozen times is my own journal."

"You keep a journal?" Julie asked.

"I started about five years ago," Brian said, nodding. "It's a great way to express all the feelings you don't really want to talk about, and it's less chancy than telling a friend and hoping he—or she—understands. I also use it to figure out how to handle tough situations." He grinned. "If I didn't, I'd probably go around mumbling to myself all the time, and then what would people think?"

"You have a point," Julie said, giggling. For a moment they were silent, gazing into the water. *Since Brian keeps a journal,* she thought suddenly, *maybe he would understand about my poetry.* "I guess my poetry does the same thing for me. It helps me express my feelings, I mean," she murmured.

"Poetry? You write poetry?"

Julie's cheeks flushed at the genuine interest in his voice. "Sometimes," she admitted.

"That's cool," Brian exclaimed. "Would you let me read some of it?"

"Well, I don't know." She hesitated. "Usually, I don't let anyone see my poems."

Brian's face fell, and he let go of her hand. "Well, if you change your mind, I'd love to see what you've written."

Now Julie wished she hadn't brought the subject up. She hadn't wanted to disappoint him, and apparently that's what she had done. But she just didn't know Brian well enough to let him read her poems. She'd never even shown them to Mary or Trisha. What if he didn't like them? What if he criticized them the way he had her article?

"Maybe we should be getting back. I can hear that lunch basket calling me," Brian said. His smile seemed a little forced to Julie.

Julie wasn't sure whether it was the word "lunch," or because Harvey was getting bored, but he wistfully looked back at them and wagged his tail. "I think it's calling your dog, too," she said with a chuckle.

"Harvey's always hungry," Brian agreed, this time with a genuine smile.

When they got back to the blanket, Brian took the food out of the cooler—thick deli sandwiches, sliced tomatoes, potato salad, and soft drinks. "This is terrific!" Julie exclaimed. "Did you make this all yourself?"

"Well, I made the sandwiches, and sliced the tomatoes," Brian said. "But Mom made the potato salad. I'm not much of a cook."

"Neither am I," Julie confessed. "I had to have help with the dessert."

"By the way, what is it?" Brian asked, eyeing the cooler with interest.

"You'll see," Julie said. "*After* lunch." She looked at Harvey, who was wagging his tail hopefully. "Can I give him a bite of my sandwich?"

"Sure. He shouldn't have it, but I can't help spoiling him. He'll eat anything. That's why he's so overweight."

Julie broke off a piece of her sandwich and handed it to Harvey. He wolfed it down and edged closer to her, drooling and wagging his tail. By the time lunch was finished, Harvey had managed to beg nearly half a sandwich between the two of them, plus the remains of the potato salad and even a tomato slice.

"He's a canine garbage can!" Julie said with a giggle.

"Yeah. And he hates exercise. When I go swimming, I can't get him into the water."

"Do you like to swim?" Julie asked with interest.

"Yes, but I like waterskiing better."

51

"Waterskiing is fun," Julie agreed. "Do you go often?"

"Almost every weekend during the summer. Dad bought a boat two years ago, and that's when I learned. How about you?"

Julie laughed. "I'm lucky if I go three or four times a year. My aunt and uncle have a summer place on a lake, and we usually go there for vacation. I'm looking forward to winter, though. I prefer skiing on snow."

"My family's into that, too. Maybe you could go with us sometime," Brian suggested. "If you can put up with my kid brothers, that is."

"How many do you have?"

"Two." Brian grimaced. "They're funny, but they can be real brats, too."

"I bet I could stand them," Julie said. "I don't have any brothers or sisters, so I usually enjoy kids."

"I don't know. My brothers are pretty tough." He rolled his eyes, then smiled. "Now, what's for dessert?"

His eyes widened when Julie unwrapped the cookies. "They look wonderful!" He reached for one and ate half of it in one bite. "Mmmm. These are delicious, Julie."

Julie nibbled at a cookie, watching in amazement as Brian devoured one after another, pausing occasionally to give Harvey a bite. Then they both started on the strawberries.

"That was great," Brian finally said with a contented sigh. "If I didn't have to go home and face my math homework, everything would be perfect."

"You don't like math either?" Julie asked. "Algebra was the worst, but geometry's not much fun either."

"Just wait until next year. Even the thought of trigonometry makes my head ache."

They leaned back against the trunk of the tree, and Brian draped an arm around her shoulders. Julie could hardly believe how much they had in common. They both liked to write, they both liked the water, and they both hated math!

"I think Harvey needs some exercise," Brian said after a few minutes of comfortable silence. He stood up and walked over to the car. A moment later he came back with a Frisbee. "Come on, Harv! Want to play?" he called.

The dog just looked up at him and didn't budge.

"Give him a little push, Julie," Brian suggested.

Julie gave Harvey's rear end a gentle shove, and he edged forward on his belly. But he didn't stand up.

"Come on, boy. *Fetch!*" Brian threw the Frisbee and pointed.

Harvey rolled over instead, waving all four feet in the air. Laughing, Julie bent down and scratched his tummy. "You're wasting your time, Brian."

"And *you're* not helping any," Brian said, smiling at her. Then he ran off to fetch the Frisbee himself.

They did manage to coax the dog into following them on another walk along the creek before they left, where Brian slipped his arm around Julie's waist.

By the time he dropped her at her front door, Julie was sure of one thing. The more she saw of Brian, the more she liked him. And even better, he seemed to like her, too.

Chapter Five

"Did he kiss you?" Trisha asked eagerly on Tuesday.

The girls were sitting alone at one of the long tables in the school cafeteria. Julie was relieved that the rest of the cheerleading squad had already left. Trisha would have probably just blurted out the embarrassing question in front of everyone.

"Of course not!" She felt her cheeks burning and almost wished she'd never told Trisha about Brian. "It was just a picnic."

"Just a picnic, nothing. It was a *date*!" Trisha exclaimed. "Did he ask you out again?"

"Not exactly," Julie said. "He asked me if I'd

like to go skiing with his family sometime, but he didn't set a date."

"Oh." Trisha frowned. "He didn't ask you out to a movie or anything?"

"No, nothing like that." Julie had been a little disappointed that Brian hadn't asked her for a second date, but she'd decided not to worry about it. After all, they'd just met. There was plenty of time.

"Too bad," Trisha sighed. "The Fall Jubilee is coming up, you know."

"How could I forget? It's all you ever talk about," Julie said. Listening to Trisha go on about the dance reminded her that she didn't have a date for the Fall Jubilee, but Julie tried to convince herself that it wasn't the end of the world. "How about you?" she asked. "Do you have a date?"

Trisha shrugged. "Danny Harris asked me, but I haven't given him an answer yet. I'm kind of hoping Frank Roberts will invite me to go with him."

Frank was the football team's starting quarterback, but there was nothing wrong with Danny either. In fact, Julie actually thought he was much nicer than Frank. "Isn't it kind of unfair not to give Danny an answer?" she asked. "I mean, if you turn him down at the last minute, he might not be able to get another date, and maybe you won't either."

"I know." Trisha looked distressed. "I figured if Frank doesn't come through today, I'll tell Danny I'll go with him. Well, guess we'd better get to class." She started to pick up her tray.

"Julie, can I talk to you a minute?"

Julie looked up and found herself staring straight into Brian's eyes. Her heart pounded.

"Sure, Brian. What is it?"

Brian straddled the bench and threw a questioning glance at Trisha.

Trisha grinned. "Don't worry. I can take a hint. I was just leaving. Don't be late for class, you two."

"We won't," Brian assured her. As soon as Trisha left he turned back to Julie. "I know you hate being late for anything, but this will just take a second."

"That's what you always say," Julie said, laughing.

He smiled a little ruefully. "I know. Believe it or not, I really *do* try to be on time. It's just that there are always so many things to do." Brian cleared his throat. "Anyway, I was wondering if—uh, if you would like to go to the Fall Jubilee with me."

Julie could hardly believe her ears. Her heart seemed to stop, then thudded wildly in her chest.

"I know it's kind of short notice," Brian said when she didn't speak. "If you already have a date, I'll understand. . . ."

57

That shook her out of her trance. "Oh, no!" she exclaimed. "I'd love to go!"

"Great." His face lit up in a smile. "I'll walk you to your next class."

Julie could hardly concentrate in the rest of her afternoon classes. For all she heard, her teachers might have been speaking Greek. All she could think about was that Brian had asked her to the Fall Jubilee. She couldn't wait to tell Trisha, and to write to Mary. She would be careful about what she wrote, though, in case Mary didn't have a boyfriend yet.

Julie was sitting at the kitchen table, flipping through several fashion magazines she had bought on the way home from school when Mrs. Davis walked in the back door.

"Hi, Mom. How was work?" Julie asked, looking up.

"Just the usual." Mrs. Davis sighed.

"Rough day?" Julie asked, realizing that her mother sounded depressed.

"Kind of," Mrs. Davis admitted. "Do you remember me telling you about Mike?"

"He's a slow learner, isn't he?"

"Yes. We had him in a Special Ed program, but it was still too difficult for him. He's so frustrated that he's been playing sick so he won't have to go to class. We'll have to move him to a sheltered workshop."

"Maybe he'll be happier there, Mom," Julie suggested.

"I hope so. He's such a nice boy." Mrs. Davis sighed again, then sat down at the table across from her daughter. "So how about you?" she asked forcing a smile. "Did you have a good day?"

Julie brightened immediately. "The best! Brian invited me to the Fall Jubilee!"

"Julie, that's wonderful," Mrs. Davis exclaimed, genuinely pleased. "Is that why you're going through all those fashion magazines?"

"I was just trying to get some ideas for a dress. Isn't this one pretty?" Julie held up a picture of a black, strapless formal.

"It looks a little old for you," her mother said dubiously.

Julie giggled. "Oh, I know that. I'd look ridiculous in something like that, but it's still pretty."

"I'll tell you what. We'll go shopping this weekend and find you the perfect dress, even if we have to go to every dress shop in Davenport."

"Really?" Impulsively, Julie jumped up and gave her mother a hug. "Oh, Mom, thanks! You're the best!"

The following day after school, Julie, Trisha, and their friends managed to snag the biggest booth at Dairy Queen, but they were still crowded in the long seat. The whole cheerleading squad was there, and Julie had invited Lisa to join them.

"Who's going to the Fall Jubilee?" Trisha asked.

"I'm going with Brad Stevens," Melanie told the group.

"Michael Parker asked me," Laura said proudly.

"Donnie and I are going, of course," Sheri said with an exaggerated sigh.

"Of course you are," another cheerleader said, laughing. "You two go everywhere together."

"And Julie is going with *Brian Frederickson*," Trisha announced dramatically.

"Lucky duck!" Sheri said enviously.

Lisa looked surprised. "I didn't know you two were seeing each other."

Julie felt her cheeks warming and wished for the thousandth time that she didn't blush so easily. "It's only our second date," she mumbled. "Are you going to the dance?" she quickly asked.

Lisa smiled and nodded. "Tim Black asked me yesterday."

"He's a reporter on the newspaper, too, isn't he?" Melanie asked. "At least you two will have something to talk about. I hardly know Brad."

"What about you, Alice?" Trisha asked the pretty Asian girl.

Alice avoided her eyes. "I'm . . . I'm going with Frank Roberts," she murmured. Sheri and Melanie exchanged knowing glances, but no one looked directly at Trisha. Julie held her breath, expecting Trisha to explode.

"That's great!" Trisha exclaimed instead.

"It is?" Alice stared at Trisha. "You're not mad? I thought you liked Frank."

Trisha chuckled. "I was interested in him for a while, but that's all in the past. Danny's the guy for me. Yesterday I told him I'd go to the dance with him, and he invited me to a movie this weekend, too."

"That's wonderful," Julie cried. "Danny was in my English class last year, and I thought he was really nice. What movie are you going to see?"

Trisha blinked. "I forgot to ask!" she admitted, giggling.

"Well, will you look at this!" a deep voice exclaimed. "All the prettiest girls in school, right in one spot!"

It was Brian. His smile seemed to take in the whole table, but his eyes were fastened on Julie. Her stomach fluttered nervously as she returned his smile.

He reached over her shoulder, plucked three french fries out of her basket, and popped them into his mouth.

"What do you think you're doing?" Julie scolded, laughing.

"Me?" he said, smiling innocently.

"Want to join us? We can make room," Sheri offered.

He shook his head. "Thanks, but the seven of you barely fit in that booth now. I just dropped by to see if Julie needs a ride home."

Julie's heart fluttered. Brian's stopping by Dairy Queen for her was like announcing to the world that they were a couple. She just hoped she wouldn't be so nervous that she'd get all tongue-tied once they were alone in his car.

"I suppose I should be getting home," she said, hoping she sounded cool. "I have tons of homework tonight."

"I'll just bet you do!" Trisha whispered loudly as the girls scrambled to let her out of the booth.

Julie made a face at her. "See you all tomorrow," she said, picking up her books and following Brian out the door.

As soon as they were outside, Brian grabbed her books out of her arms and gently took her hand. "I'm always surprised when I see you with Trisha and the other cheerleaders," he said.

"Why? What's wrong with them?" Julie asked, annoyed. She hoped he wasn't going to say anything bad about her friends, or about her. What if he thought she wasn't pretty or popular enough to be hanging around with them?

"Nothing," he said quickly. "Don't get so defensive! They're a lot of fun. It's just that you seem, well, quieter, more thoughtful, than the rest of them."

"Maybe I am," Julie admitted. "We don't have a lot in common, but I really like them, especially Trisha. She gets me to try things I probably wouldn't do on my own."

"Like go out for the *Gazette*?" Brian asked with a grin.

"Exactly."

"Well, I'm glad you did." He squeezed her fingers, then let go of her hand as he opened the car door for her. "If you hadn't, I might never have gotten to know you."

Julie felt a warm glow spreading through her. Brian made her feel so special! *But we don't know each other very well,* she reminded herself. She'd better not let her daydreams get out of hand, or she might end up disappointed.

"By the way, have you come up with a subject for your next column?" Brian asked as he drove out of the parking lot.

"As a matter of fact, I have," Julie said. Then she hesitated. Would he approve of her idea, or would he veto it like he had the last time? That idea about the school library had been her fourth choice.

Brian glanced over at her, grinning. "What is it? Or am I supposed to guess?"

"I thought I'd write about the girls' athletic program." She held her breath, hoping he'd like it.

"That sounds terrific," he said enthusiastically. "I don't think anyone has ever done a piece on that subject. If you need any help, just let me know."

"Okay," Julie said, breathing a sigh of relief. "I will."

A few minutes later they pulled up in front of her house. Brian hopped out and came around to her side of the car. Although it felt a little weird, Julie made herself wait until he opened the door. This business of being treated like a lady took some getting used to, but it certainly was enjoyable!

Brian walked her to the front door. Since he wasn't in a hurry to leave, they stood on the porch for a while and talked about school. Then he asked Julie a lot of questions about her family, including some he'd asked before. He seemed nervous for some reason. She didn't know what to make of Brian's odd behavior, so she invited him in, but he shook his head. "I'd better get going. I have a lot of homework tonight, too," he said. He shifted from one foot to the other, then suddenly leaned forward and quickly kissed her on the cheek.

"See you tomorrow," he mumbled, then turned and trotted back to his car.

Julie just stood there for a second, watching him drive away until the car was out of sight. Wonderingly, she touched the spot on her cheek where he'd kissed her. It still felt warm, although she knew that must be her imagination.

Julie smiled dreamily. Brian must like her a lot, or he wouldn't have been so nervous about kissing her. She really liked him, too, despite their former differences over her column. He was the most wonderful boy Julie had ever known, and she could hardly wait for the Fall Jubilee!

Chapter Six

The next day, Julie began interviewing several of Memorial High's top female athletes.

"So you have to buy your own rackets?" she asked.

"The only thing the school pays for is the tennis balls. They do give us those ratty, old uniforms though," the captain of the girls' tennis team said.

"They buy our uniforms and shoes, too," said the star catcher on the girls' softball team.

"I think they buy everyone's uniforms," said a member of the swim team. "We get our team swimsuits free."

"Yes, but the boys' basketball team has had

their stuff replaced *twice* since the girls got new uniforms," a member of the girls' basketball team pointed out.

"I don't mind that so much. The boys are a lot rougher on their stuff than we are," said a star of the track team. "What really bothers me is that if you're a girl, you only have five interscholastic sports to choose from. The boys have eight. I played soccer all through junior high, and I was good, too. Then when I got to high school, there was no girls' soccer team!"

"But, of course, there's a *boys'* team," the softball catcher added.

"Football, soccer, and wrestling," said the swimmer. "Those are all boys only."

"I don't imagine many girls would want to play football or wrestle," Julie commented as her pencil flew across her notebook page.

"True, but there should be something to take their place. Volleyball, for instance. Or gymnastics," the track star said. "I took years of gymnastics lessons, and my teacher said I was pretty good. If we had a program here at school, I might have had a chance at a scholarship."

Another basketball player spoke up for the first time. "There's another thing that burns me. Last year the girls' basketball team won the state championship, yet we only got to stay overnight once—during the finals. Every other time they bused us back the same night. My boyfriend is on the boys' team, and they got to stay overnight four times!"

"That's not fair!" said another.

"You want to talk about unfair?" the tennis captain broke in. "Then let's talk football. Do you know how many guys there are on the football team? Nearly as many as in all the other sports combined. That means almost *twice* as many boys get to compete as girls."

"Right. And the football team gets all kinds of privileges. Overnight road trips, cheerleaders, pep rallies . . . I'll bet over half the sports budget goes to the football team alone!" the runner said.

"Are you sure of that?" Julie asked. She could hardly believe her ears. It seemed that sexual discrimination was alive and well at Memorial High, even though the teachers were always talking about how things were equal now, and that girls could be and do whatever they wanted, just like boys.

"I'm not one hundred percent positive, but it shouldn't be too hard to check. You might try talking to some of the coaches, or the principal," the other girl said.

Julie cornered the girls' basketball coach and head of the girls' athletic program during her free period. "Mrs. Norton, could I talk to you for a minute?" she asked. "I'm Julie Davis, and I write a column for the *Gazette*."

"Why, certainly," Mrs. Norton said with a smile.

Mrs. Norton was a petite, pretty woman with reddish-brown hair. In her slim skirt and high heels, it was hard for Julie to imagine her coaching a championship basketball team, but she realized that you couldn't really tell much about people from the way they looked. She led Julie to her small office at the back of the girls' locker room and asked, "What can I do for you?"

"I'm writing an article about the girls' athletic program," Julie explained.

"That's great! Everyone tends to focus on the boys, and forgets all about us. What can I tell you?"

"Do you think the girls' athletic programs get a fair shake?" Julie asked, her pencil in hand.

"In what way?" A look of caution replaced Mrs. Norton's smile.

"Oh, I don't know. . . ." Julie tried to look nonchalant, knowing that a good reporter should put her subject at ease. That way, the person would be more likely to say something interesting—at least, that's what the book she'd gotten from the library said. "It's just that I've heard a few complaints about the girls' program."

Mrs. Norton frowned. "Could you be more specific?"

69

"Well, there are several things. Some of the girls think the boys get more and better equipment than they do, and special privileges. There's also some concern about the smaller number of sports programs available to girls. For instance, there's no girls' soccer or volleyball team."

"Are you going to quote me?" Mrs. Norton asked.

"I write an opinion column, so there's really no reason to use names," Julie told her. "I could just say I got my information from an 'informed source.' "

"That would be fine. I get enough flak as it is." Mrs. Norton relaxed a little. "Everything you've heard is true. I have to practically beg to get new uniforms for my girls, even though the boys' basketball team gets new ones every other year. And that's just one example."

"Could you give me some others?" Julie asked eagerly.

"Sure. Travel budgets. With some of the sports, like swimming, the team is coed, so the boys and girls are treated more equally. But when it comes to segregated sports, like basketball, baseball, and football, it's a different story. We almost always bring the girls home after a basketball game, no matter how far away it is, because we just don't have the money for motel accommodations. The PTA had to come up with part of the money when the girls went to Des Moines for the finals last year."

Julie nodded, writing fast. "Are there any other major differences?" she asked.

"Coaching," Mrs. Norton answered promptly. "For football, baseball, and boys' basketball, a coach is hired, and assigned to teach a class or two, usually P.E., on top of his coaching responsibilities. But for girls' sports, they usually assign a regular teacher who happens to be interested in the sport."

"I see," Julie said. "Hold on just a second while I get this all down."

"That's not all," Mrs. Norton said after a pause. "Salary also has an impact on the quality of coaching. Women coaches make less money."

"But that's not fair!" Julie said, astonished.

"You're telling me," Mrs. Norton said bitterly. "Well, it's almost time for my next class, Julie. I hope this helps with your column."

"It sure will, Mrs. Norton. Thank you!" Julie stood up.

"Remember not to use my name!" the teacher called after her as she left the office.

Julie was so angry because of what she had just learned that she waited until the next day to make an appointment with Mr. Bentley, the principal. It wouldn't do any good to lose her temper and start yelling at him, and that was exactly what she feared would happen if she

71

saw him right away. She knew she mustn't reveal how upset she was, or he might not let her see the records she needed.

By the time Julie was sitting in Mr. Bentley's office the next day, she felt perfectly calm, at least on the outside. She only hoped she could stay that way.

"I'm doing a piece on the school athletic programs for the *Gazette*, Mr. Bentley," she said sweetly. "I was hoping you could fill in a few blanks for me."

"Glad to help, Julie." He smiled broadly at her. The fluorescent light glistened on his bald head. "I'm a real sports fan myself. Never miss a football or baseball game if I can help it."

Julie controlled an urge to ask if he ever attended any of the girls' games, and if not, why not. She knew he'd never give her the information she wanted if she antagonized him. That was why she hadn't said she was writing about the girls' sports program in particular.

"Mostly, I need some figures," she said. "I'm interested in the budget for interscholastic sports."

"No problem," he said, standing up and opening a filing cabinet. "Do you need a summary, or an itemized budget?"

"I'm not sure," she said. "What I really want is a breakdown by sport."

"I'll give you both, then." He pulled some

sheets of paper out of the cabinet. "Wait here while I make copies."

While he was gone, Julie glanced around the room. She had never been sent to the principal's office for disciplinary reasons, but she had always regarded it as an intimidating place. Now it felt good sitting here as if she belonged, having Mr. Bentley rushing around trying to please her.

A momentary feeling of power flowed through her, but nervousness quickly took over. Mrs. Norton had been so worried about making waves that she didn't want her name used. Julie, however, would be putting *her* name right on the bottom of her column. If Mr. Bentley didn't like what she wrote, she could find herself here again, under much less pleasant circumstances.

The principal walked back in before she could scare herself any more, and handed her several sheets of paper. "Take a look at the figures before you leave," he suggested. "If they don't tell you everything you need to know, I'll be happy to answer your questions."

Julie quickly scanned the numbers. Her friends had been right about the huge football budget. It was more than twice the size of the budget for any other sport. The next biggest was boys' basketball, then baseball. Girls' basketball and the other sports trailed far behind.

"Why is the football budget so big?" Julie asked innocently.

"Two reasons." Mr. Bentley spoke so quickly that Julie wondered if he'd been asked that question before. "First, there are a lot of football players. Second, football takes a lot of expensive equipment."

"All that protective gear, huh? That makes sense." Julie made herself smile, then glanced at the figures again. "Hmm—I see the boys' basketball team has a much bigger budget than the girls'."

"That's because the guys are harder on equipment and uniforms than the girls are. Boys' basketball is a rougher game—you know how boys are." Mr. Bentley chuckled.

Julie didn't buy that, but she let it pass. "Does boys' baseball use more equipment than girls' softball?" she asked.

Mr. Bentley's smile faded, and he eyed her warily. "Just what are you getting at?" he asked.

Julie shrugged. "I was just wondering why all the boys' sports seem to have bigger budgets than the girls'."

"It's all a matter of economics, Julie," the principal said.

"I guess I don't understand." She tried her best to look innocent and confused. "What does economics have to do with how much the school spends on sports equipment?"

Mr. Bentley sighed. "It's really quite simple. Boys' sports draw bigger crowds than girls' sports, so they make more in admissions and concession revenues," he explained.

"Then that money is spent on the program that produced it?"

"Not exactly." Julie noticed how uncomfortable the principal looked. "But that's not the only reason for the differences."

"What's the other reason?"

"Scholarships. Big college scholarships are available in football and boys' basketball."

"Don't some colleges offer girls' athletic scholarships?" Julie prodded.

"Well, yes, they do." He ran a hand over his bald head. "There's not nearly as much money involved, though."

"So that's why Memorial High concentrates on the boys."

"Basically, yes. Everyone benefits when our students get their share of available scholarships."

"Everyone except the girls," Julie said, gritting her teeth. "Isn't that a little unfair?"

"It may seem that way, but it's not our fault," Mr. Bentley blustered. "If anyone is to blame, it's the universities that offer those scholarships. If they'd put more emphasis on women's sports, then we would, too."

"I see." Julie stood up, clutching the budget and her notebook. "Well, thank you for explaining everything to me. It's been very . . . *educational.*"

She could feel Mr. Bentley staring at her as she left the office.

Julie stared at her printed column in disbelief on Monday morning. This wasn't what she had written at all! Her eyes widened as she read on. Someone had cut out all the good parts. They'd rewritten the whole thing without even bothering to consult her!

Brian hadn't suggested they go over her article when she had handed it in. He'd driven her home from school on Friday afternoon and hadn't said a single word about a rewrite, either. Julie had wanted to ask how he'd liked her column, but she had decided against it. What if he hated it and they had another fight right before the dance?

Of course, Brian's criticism had made her previous column much better than her original piece, but this was different! This time someone had ripped her work to pieces and put it back together all wrong. Who could it be but Brian?

Instead of toning down the strong language, he had simply chopped it out. By the time he was finished, the female athletes sounded like a bunch of whiners. Julie would be lucky if any of those girls ever spoke to her again.

She forced herself to read the column once

more, holding back tears of rage. Reading it again made it even worse. Then she read the rest of the paper extra carefully, to see if any of the other articles had gotten so drastically cut. But they all seemed perfectly normal, not chopped up and disjointed like hers.

Julie couldn't believe it. She had thought Brian was her friend—actually, much more than a friend. Even though it wasn't exactly official, she'd begun to think of him as her boyfriend. How could he do something as awful as this? And she was supposed to go to the Fall Jubilee with him this Saturday! What was she going to do?

Chapter Seven

"Brian didn't say one word about what he did to my column," Julie complained, pacing back and forth across Trisha's bedroom. "He even drove me home from school on Friday! We went out Saturday night, and he called on Sunday, and he still didn't mention it!"

Trisha took a handful of chips out of the bag she was holding, then passed it to Julie. "Mom doesn't like for me to eat in here, so don't drop any, and try not to spill any soda, okay?" she said. Trisha's mother was an interior decorator who redecorated the entire house every couple of years. Although Trisha didn't seem to mind her quirks, Julie sometimes felt a little sorry for her friend. Today, however, she didn't feel sorry for anybody except herself.

Julie set her glass down very carefully and helped herself to some chips. "So what do you think?"

"About Brian?" Trisha asked, munching. "I don't see what the big deal is. So he rewrote your article a little. That's his job."

"He didn't rewrite it a *little*. He *mangled* it! I could hardly tell it was the same piece I gave him!"

Trisha raised one eyebrow. "Are you sure you're not exaggerating?"

"Of course I'm sure. Here, listen to this!" Julie picked up her notebook and opened it. "This is what I wrote. 'When it comes to money, female athletes suffer even more. The boys' athletic program receives three dollars for every dollar spent on the girls' program. Although Mr. Bentley justifies this inequality because of the larger number of male athletes, that is obviously just a cover-up for Memorial High's blatant sexual discrimination. Otherwise, why would the boys' basketball team have gotten two new sets of uniforms since the girls' uniforms were replaced?' "

Julie threw down the notebook and picked up her copy of the *Gazette*. "Now listen to what *he* wrote. 'The girls' athletic program gets one dollar for every three spent on the boys. Although this might seem unfair, Mr.

Bentley points out that many more boys than girls participate in sports and their equipment is more expensive.' "

Trisha grimaced. "That does sort of miss the point," she admitted.

"*Sort of?* It makes it sound like there's no problem except that the girls like to complain!" Julie tossed the newspaper onto Trisha's puffy green bedspread and ate another chip.

"Maybe it was just a mistake," Trisha suggested.

"Oh sure," Julie said sarcastically and gave her friend a disgusted look. "Brian accidentally lost my article so he wrote this piece of garbage and put it in the paper instead. I tell you, Trisha, he's picking on me. I'll bet he doesn't rewrite any of the others' stuff like he does mine."

"But Julie," Trisha objected, "why would he pick on you? He acts like he's crazy about you."

"Maybe he's just pretending. Maybe I did something to make him mad when we went on that picnic," Julie worried.

"That doesn't make any sense," Trisha said firmly, stretching out on the bed beside her. "If he didn't really like you, why would he drive you home from school, and take you out, and invite you to the Fall Jubilee?"

"I don't know," Julie admitted. Then she

thought, *Maybe he is hurt because I won't let him read my poetry.* Well, after what Brian had just done to her column, she was glad she hadn't shared her personal poems with him. He would probably have just picked them apart, too.

"You'd better talk to him about it soon," Trisha said. "You have to spend the whole evening with him this Saturday, remember? It won't be much fun if you're mad."

"That is, if I go," Julie said, scowling.

Trisha immediately sat upright, looking horrified. "Of course you're going! Don't even *think* of backing out! This is the biggest dance of the year, and it's too late to get another date!"

Julie couldn't help smiling at her friend's reaction. Trust Trisha to put a party ahead of everything, even something as serious as Brian's betrayal. She should have known that Trisha wouldn't understand how strongly she felt about it.

The best thing she could do now was change the subject before she ended up being mad at Trisha, too. "Speaking of which, do you have your dress yet?" Julie asked.

"Do I! Wait till you see it!" Trisha ran over to her walk-in closet, grabbed a hanger and whirled around, holding an exquisite dress in front of her. "Ta-da!"

It was a dark metallic green, off-the-shoulder dress with a short, full skirt.

81

"It's beautiful, Trisha, but . . ." Suddenly Julie giggled.

"But what?" Trisha asked, frowning.

"It looks so sophisticated. You're going to scare Danny to death!"

"I hope so." Now Trisha giggled, too. "It'll do him good!"

As she walked home a while later, Julie's thoughts returned to the dance. She just didn't know if she could bring herself to go with Brian, despite Trisha's insistence. What would they talk about? How terrible her column was? How he planned to mutilate her next column? Having a big fight at the dance would be worse than not going at all.

Julie's mother was in the kitchen when she got home.

"You're home early, Mom," Julie said.

"Yes, we had a seminar, and it finished a little sooner than I expected."

"How was it?"

"Boring." Mrs. Davis smiled. "They usually are, but I did learn a couple of things, and I got to catch up with some old friends." She looked at Julie closely. "So how was your day, honey? You look like you could use some cheering up."

"It was awful, Mom, just awful." The tears Julie had managed to hold back all day now began to spill over.

"What's wrong, Julie?" Mrs. Davis hurried

over to her daughter. She put her arm around Julie's shoulders and led her into the family room.

Julie slumped down on the brown tweed sofa beside her mother. "It was the worst day of my entire life," she cried. Through her tears she managed to pour out the story of how Brian had mangled her column.

"I understand how you feel, honey," Mrs. Davis said trying to comfort Julie. "I was afraid something like this would happen, but maybe it was just a misunderstanding. What did Brian have to say about it?"

"I haven't even talked to him about it. What could I possibly say after what he did?" Julie said indignantly.

Mrs. Davis sighed. "Julie, problems don't get solved if you don't deal with them. How will you avoid a problem on your next column if you and Brian don't discuss what went wrong on this one?"

"But I just can't!" Julie moaned. "Anyway, that stupid column is the least of my worries. I'm supposed to go to the dance with him on Saturday—unless, of course, I decide to cancel."

"Well, Julie, that's a decision that only you can make, and I know you will give it some thought before you do."

Julie considered the beautiful, red-trimmed white formal hanging in the closet in the spare room, so it wouldn't get crushed. It made her look so grown-up, and with her new red satin pumps, and the satin-and-lace comb for her hair . . . She sniffled miserably. "If I don't go, I'll just spend Saturday night crying."

"If you *do* go, at least you'll be with your friends," Mrs. Davis pointed out.

Julie took a deep breath. "That's true." *And I won't have to worry about explaining why I didn't show up,* she thought. *That ought to teach me to keep my big mouth shut! I told* everyone *I was going with Brian.*

"There are Brian's feeling to consider, too," her mother said gently. "If you back out three days before the dance, he may not be able to get another date. That wouldn't really be fair."

Julie frowned. "He didn't think about *my* feelings when he butchered my article. But I guess you're right—finding another date this late would be a problem. All the girls I know already are going with someone."

"Do you think another boy might ask you to the dance if you cancel your date with Brian?" Mrs. Davis asked.

"Not a chance," Julie said glumly. "Besides, if either one of us showed up with someone else, people would ask a lot of embarrassing questions."

"So by staying home you can put off the awkward questions until Monday," her mother said, half smiling.

"Monday! That would be even worse!" Julie cried. "There's just no way I can back out. I'm better off going, even if I have a miserable time. Besides, I told him I would, and it wouldn't be right to go back on my word."

Mrs. Davis nodded. "Good decision. Who knows? Maybe you'll have fun in spite of this. But honey, I really think you should talk to him about the column before the dance."

"I don't know," Julie said with a sigh. "It might just make things worse between us."

"On the other hand it might clear everything up," her mother said. "Give Brian a chance to tell his side of the story. You may find out that it's quite different from what you suppose."

"I'll think about it," Julie promised, though she doubted she would do more than think. If he said anything cruel about her writing, she just wouldn't be able to stand it.

Chapter Eight

By Saturday evening, Julie still hadn't spoken to Brian about her column. She glared at her reflection in the mirror, thinking that the dress hadn't seemed This loose in the store. She had always been satisfied with her slim figure, but suddenly she wished she were a little more developed on top, just enough to fill out the gown's bodice properly.

She took a deep breath, and for a moment the red velvet top fit perfectly. Too bad she couldn't hold her breath all evening!

The rest of the dress did look wonderful. The full, flowing white skirt just skimmed the tops of her satin pumps. Though the neckline was demure in front, it dipped way down in back.

Julie looked in the mirror and for once she truly felt pretty. Her mother had helped her curl her short, brown hair, and Julie had added the lace-trimmed comb they had bought. She was wearing bright red lipstick, sparkly gold eye shadow, and mascara. She hardly recognized herself.

Julie sighed deeply. All of this for a boy she'd been avoiding all week. Avoiding Brian hadn't been easy either. She had stopped going to Dairy Queen with Trisha and her friends because she was sure Brian would stop by and ask if she needed a lift. She hadn't run into him in the halls at school, and there hadn't been a newspaper meeting. Maybe it was silly, but Julie didn't want to risk an argument before the dance, and she knew that if she saw him, she'd probably blow up.

Brian had called twice, though, once to remind her of their date and the second time to ask what color her dress was. But he never once referred to her column, let alone apologized for it.

Still, in spite of everything, Julie had been determined to at least pretend to have a good time at the dance—until the ring of the doorbell sent her into a panic. What if Brian was angry because she hadn't been riding home with him? What if he disliked her dress as much as he had disliked her column?

Suddenly she wished she had canceled their date.

Julie forced herself to take a deep breath and calm down. It was too late to back out now. Taking one last glance at her reflection in the mirror, she held her head high and walked downstairs confidently.

When she came into the living room, she saw Brian standing with his back to her, talking to her parents. He was wearing a dark blue suit, and even from behind, Julie could tell he looked handsome.

"Uh—hi," Julie said softly.

Brian turned around, and when he saw her, his eyes widened and a smile spread across his face. He stared at her for so long that Julie began to wonder if something was wrong. "Julie, you look beautiful!" he whispered at last.

Julie smiled, too. "Surprised?" she asked.

"Yes! Uh, I mean no . . ." Brian blushed. "You're always pretty, but today you look—perfect."

"Thank you." Julie knew she was blushing, too. That was the nicest thing anyone had ever said to her. For a moment, she almost forgot to be angry with Brian. Then it all came back in a rush.

"You do look lovely, dear," Mrs. Davis said, and Mr. Davis agreed.

"Well, kids, have a good time," he said. "Take good care of my little girl, Brian."

Julie cringed at being called a little girl, but Brian just nodded solemnly. "Don't worry, I will," he promised. Then he turned to Julie. "This is for you," he said, holding out a corsage.

She caught her breath. One perfect white rose was nestled in lacy ferns, held by a red velvet bow. "Thank you," she murmured.

After Julie put on her coat, Brian fastened the corsage to her dress, fumbling with the long pins. Julie hoped he wouldn't stab her. He seemed nervous enough to do just that—at least she wasn't the only one who was nervous.

As he helped her into his car a few minutes later, Brian told her again how wonderful she looked. This time, instead of pleasing her his compliment made her angry. He probably thought that flattery would make up for the way he had butchered her article. She had to press her lips together to keep from telling him that it wasn't going to work.

Julie sat stiffly on her side of the car, her hands folded tightly in her lap. They rode in silence for a while.

"Where have you been lately, Julie?" Brian finally asked. "I looked for you around school Thursday and Friday, but I didn't see you anywhere."

Julie stared straight ahead. "I've been pretty busy. I have an English paper due next week."

That was true, even if it wasn't the *whole* truth.

"I'm glad to hear that," Brian said, smiling. "I was afraid you were mad at me about your column."

"Oh, really?" Julie clenched her fists, no longer able to control the anger that had been building all week. He wanted to know if she was mad? Well, she was more than happy to tell him. "Whatever gave you that idea?" she snapped. "Just because you took a good, strong article and turned it into disgusting mush, why should I be mad? Why should I care about what you did to the column I slaved over?"

"I thought so," Brian said and sighed.

"Well, what did you expect?" Julie yelled. "I mean, even if you *hated* it, at least you could have talked to me about it before you ripped it to shreds!"

"I'm really sorry," he mumbled.

"Well, you should be." Julie sniffed, looking away.

"I am. I've been worrying about it all week." Brian frowned. "I was running so far behind that I didn't get a chance to read the articles I'd gotten until the day before they had to be typeset. Your column was too long, and there were a couple of quotes from Mr. Bentley I didn't think we should print. I knew I'd miss the deadline if I gave it back to you for a rewrite, so I asked someone else to shorten it while I edited some pieces that were in really bad shape."

Julie still refused to look at him, but his explanation made her feel a little better. At least Brian hadn't done those awful revisions himself. But he must have approved them, she reminded herself, feeling her anger well up inside again. "What did you think of the result?" she asked.

Brian grimaced. "Not much. I just told Tim to shorten it and tone it down a little, but he got carried away. I didn't even have time to read his revisions until after the paper was printed, so it's truly my fault, not his. As the editor, I'm supposed to be on top of everything. What can I say? I goofed."

"Why didn't you say something when you called?" Julie asked.

"Why didn't you?" Brian countered, glancing over at her.

"It didn't seem like something to talk about on the phone," Julie mumbled, feeling uncomfortable.

Brian grinned. "That's my reason, too. I was afraid you'd hang up on me."

That made her smile, just a little. "I might have," she admitted. "I was pretty mad for a while."

"If I want a rewrite on your next column, I'll definitely tell you about it," Brian promised, "even if I completely miss the deadline."

"I'd appreciate that," Julie said softly. A warm glow spread through her as Brian reached out and took her hand. Suddenly she was really looking forward to the dance, and she silently thanked her mother for persuading her to go.

Julie hardly recognized the school gymnasium when they entered a few minutes later. A huge, mirrored ball suspended from the ceiling rotated slowly, reflecting the lights and breaking them into rainbows. Refreshment tables covered by russet tablecloths were placed at one end of the gym, each with a centerpiece of fall flowers and autumn leaves. It looked very elegant. Extra chairs had been set up on either side of the area that was cleared for dancing.

The Highwaymen, a popular rock band, was already playing, and a number of couples were dancing, while others clustered around the refreshment tables. Julie saw Trisha and Danny immediately. Trisha looked very sophisticated in the green dress with her blond hair piled on top of her head, and Danny kept stealing glances at her as if he couldn't quite believe his eyes.

"Danny seems to like your dress," Julie said, smiling, as Danny and Brian walked away to get cups of punch for the girls.

Trisha giggled. "I thought he was going to faint when he saw me. He's really nice. Last night after the movie he told me he's wanted to ask me out for *months*!"

"Why did he wait?" Julie asked.

"He thought I liked Frank. Can you believe that?" Trisha rolled her eyes.

Julie decided against pointing out that until very recently Trisha would have done just about anything to get Frank to notice her.

"So how are you and Brian doing?" Trisha asked. "Are you still mad at him about what he did to your column?"

"Oh, I'm over that," Julie said indifferently. "It was all just a silly misunderstanding."

"Really?" Trisha raised her eyebrows. "You sure didn't think so yesterday."

"I'll tell you all about it later," Julie promised. "Now let's talk about something else. Here come the guys."

"Would you like to dance, Julie?" Brian asked when they finished their punch.

Julie smiled. "I'd love to."

They danced to almost every song, and when they did sit one out, Brian put his arm around her. They talked very little, because the band was so loud, but Julie didn't mind at all. Now that everything had been cleared up, she was perfectly happy just being with him. She loved resting her head against Brian's shoulder and feeling his arms around her as they danced.

The music was still playing when they left.

"I know it's early, but I told your folks I'd have you home by midnight," Brian said as they walked to the car, "and I thought you might like to get something to eat."

"I wouldn't mind. I'm pretty sick of punch and chips," Julie told him.

Brian drove to a twenty-four-hour diner on the edge of town, where he ordered a big platter of bacon and eggs. Julie decided on a burger and fries. As they ate, they talked, and by the time they got back into his car, Julie felt as if she had known Brian's family for years. The stories he told about the tricks he'd pulled on his little brothers made her laugh until her stomach hurt.

Her own life seemed pretty dull in comparison, but Brian didn't seem to think so. He asked lots of questions about her parents' jobs, and about her friend Mary. Julie was surprised to find herself telling him things that she hadn't even shared with Trisha—like how much she still missed Mary.

Finally, Brian glanced at his watch. "I suppose I'd better get you home. It's quarter to twelve," he said with a sigh.

"That's probably a good idea," Julie agreed reluctantly. She hated to see the evening end.

Neither of them said much on the way home, although Brian held her hand. When they pulled into the Davises' driveway, he got out of the car and opened the door for Julie, then slipped his arm around her as they walked up onto the porch.

"Well, thank you for such a nice evening," Brian said very formally.

Julie smiled. "I had a lovely time." How odd that she should feel more at ease than Brian apparently did.

"Julie," he said softly, "I really enjoy being with you. Will you go out with me again?"

"I'd like that a lot." Her heart raced. He wanted to see her again! Would he kiss her now?

"Great! Well, good night." Brian removed his arm from around her waist.

That was it? Julie knew she should be content with knowing that he wanted to see her again, but she couldn't help feeling disappointed. "Good night," she echoed quietly.

"I'll call you," Brian said and slowly turned away. Then suddenly he faced her again, put his arms around her, and pulled her close like he had when they were slow dancing.

Julie slipped her arms around his neck and looked up at him, her heart pounding. Did he expect her to make the next move?

Brian bent his head and brushed his lips across her forehead. She shivered nervously and tilted her head back. He then gently kissed her lips. Her eyes started to shut, but it all ended too quickly. Brian released her and stepped back.

"Tomorrow," he said, shyly. "I'll call you tomorrow, okay?"

"I'll be waiting," Julie murmured, thinking that Brian was even more charming when he was shy.

"Are we going to be late for class, Julie?" Lisa asked on Monday afternoon as she burst into the girls' bathroom.

Julie glanced at her watch. "We still have five minutes," she said.

"Oh, good. Mrs. Norton gave us a real workout in gym today. Even after showering, I'm still boiling." Lisa vigorously brushed her long, dark brown hair. "We have a newspaper meeting after school, right?"

Julie nodded. Ever since the dance, she had been trying to figure out how she really felt about Brian. Their kiss had been wonderful, and she was pretty sure she was falling in love with him.

But she couldn't help resenting how critical he was of her columns. And why did he reject most of her ideas? Did he do that to everyone, or was he singling her out because he secretly thought she wrote poorly? Now was a good time to find out.

"So how do you like working on the *Gazette* so far?" she asked Lisa, hoping she sounded casual.

"It's a lot of work, but it's fun, too. How about you?" Lisa asked.

"I enjoy it," Julie said, "but I wish I had more time to do rewrites. Is that a problem for you?"

"Not really," Lisa said. "Most of the time the revisions aren't too major, and Brian's usually pretty clear about what he wants." She stuck her brush back in her purse. "Some of the others haven't been so lucky, though. Kim wouldn't speak to him for a week after he told her to scrap her first news piece and start all over again."

"Really?" Julie said. "Then I don't feel so bad about what he does to my stuff."

"You shouldn't feel bad at all," Lisa said. "You're a terrific writer. If Brian gives you a hard time, it's probably because you guys are dating and he doesn't want it to look like he's playing favorites."

"I never thought about it that way," Julie said slowly. "Maybe you're right." Then she glanced at her watch. "Uh-oh—now we'd better hurry or we *will* be late for class."

Chapter Nine

"**H**ow about *Romancing the Stone?*" Julie's father asked her mother that evening at supper.

"Oh, Allan," Mrs. Davis said, "we've rented that movie at least a dozen times. Let's get something we haven't seen before."

"What do you think, Julie?" Mr. Davis asked.

Julie set her fork down. "Count me out. I have some things I need to work on tonight so no time for a movie."

"Homework?" her mother asked.

"It's actually my newspaper column," Julie said.

"How is that going? Brian hasn't been giving you any more trouble, has he?" Mrs. Davis asked.

Julie shook her head. "Nope—everything's fine."

"Are you sure?" her father prodded. "You haven't eaten much of your dinner."

Julie smiled. "I had a big lunch today. Besides, I'm not all that crazy about meat loaf," she said knowing that she really was worried about Brian's reaction to her column.

As soon as the dishes were cleared and her parents left for the video store, Julie hurried upstairs. Throwing herself across her bed, she kicked off her shoes and wiggled her toes. Why was Brian so critical of everything she wrote? There must be some way to please him.

She stared up at the ceiling and thought for a long time before an idea came to her. Maybe she should spend more time on planning. If she carefully worked out how she intended to approach each topic, she'd be able to answer the questions he was bound to ask. Certainly if he approved every aspect of her project before she even began to write, he'd have to be satisfied with the final result.

Julie jumped up and ran over to her computer. It didn't take long to come up with three ideas. Turning them into project outlines was harder, but when she was finished, she had three neatly typed proposals, each with a snappy title, a list of interviewees, and the points she hoped to prove.

Julie stuck the lists in her book bag and picked

up her poetry notebook. Tuning the radio to a soft-rock station, she curled up in the chair by the window and stared at a blank sheet of paper. Then she smiled and began writing.

On Tuesday morning, Julie tried not to fidget as she waited for Brian by his locker. It was silly to be so nervous. After the dance, and that wonderful kiss, she knew he liked her. He was taking her to a movie this weekend, but what if he didn't like any of her new column ideas? After all her work, she hated the thought of his rejecting every single one.

"Julie! Hi!" Brian said and bent down to lightly kiss her cheek. Suddenly her nervousness disappeared.

"We're still on for Sunday afternoon, aren't we?" He grinned at her, and her heart pounded wildly.

"Sure. I just thought we ought to talk about my next column."

"Okay. When do you want to do it?"

"Would after school be okay?" Julie asked.

"Today?" Brian frowned.

"If that's a problem we can do it some other time," Julie said hastily. Maybe she'd been too pushy. Should she have let him suggest the time? After all, he was the editor of the *Gazette* and she was just a reporter.

"The thing is, I locked Harvey inside this morning because it was raining. My mom's

away, so I need to get home to let him out."
Then Brian's face brightened. "Hey, why don't
you ride home with me and we'll talk about
your column there?"

"That would be fine," Julie agreed.

"Great! Meet me by my car." He slipped his
arm around her shoulders and gave her a gentle squeeze. "See you after school."

Julie was afraid the day would never end,
but her classes kept her so busy that almost
before she knew it, the final bell rang. She
found Trisha waiting for her by her locker.

"Where were you at lunch?" Trisha teased.
"Holding hands with Brian?"

"I just grabbed a sandwich and left. There
were some things I had to take care of," Julie
said. She felt a little guilty because she hadn't
told Trisha she'd hurried off to go over her
ideas for the column one last time.

"Hey, no problem. Danny saw how lonely I
was and decided to keep me company." Trisha
grinned.

"You really like him, don't you?"

"Yes. Who would have thought it?" Trisha
shook her head, then patted her fluffy blond
hair. "He's not even a jock! Ready to go to
Dairy Queen?"

"Sorry. I can't go today," Julie said. "I have
to work on my column with Brian."

Trisha gave her a knowing look. "Yeah,
right. Is he a good kisser?"

"Trisha!" Julie blushed. "Listen, I've got to run. I'm supposed to meet him by his car."

"Where are you two going?" Trisha asked.

"To his house. He has to let his dog out."

Trisha hooted with laughter. "That's a new one! I'll bet you'll get a lot of work done there!"

Julie felt as if her cheeks were on fire. "Trisha, I really have to go. Brian will be wondering where I am."

"Don't get hysterical," Trisha yelled down the hall. "He's never been on time for anything in his life."

But Trisha was wrong, and Julie found Brian waiting for her by his car.

"Sorry I'm late," she gasped, a little out of breath.

"That's okay. It's kind of nice when someone else is running behind schedule for a change," Brian said smiling.

They got into the car, but when Brian turned the ignition key the engine just made a low growling sound. He frowned and pumped the gas pedal. This time the motor turned over, but a moment later it died. Finally on the fifth try it ran. Brian looked exasperated. "Must need a tune-up or something."

'I guess," Julie said doubtfully. "All I know about cars is where to put the gas."

"Don't worry. It's never failed me yet." Brian grinned at her as they drove out of the parking lot.

"So how was your day?" Julie asked.

"Just the usual. Rush, rush, rush."

"You're the busiest person I know," she said.

"I just can't seem to say no," Brian admitted. "This morning a friend of mine suckered me in to helping him build sets for the Drama Club's Christmas play. Editing the paper takes about twice as long as I expected, too."

"And now you have to take up your afternoon working on my column with me," Julie said.

Brian laughed. "Spending time with you isn't exactly a chore," he said, reaching over to squeeze her hand.

Julie smiled. "I'm glad you feel that way because I can't say it's too tough being with you either."

Brian pulled the car into the driveway of a big, red brick house with two huge fir trees in the front yard.

"What a pretty house," Julie exclaimed.

"Thanks. It's over a hundred years old," Brian said. "My mom and dad have done a lot of work on it."

He opened the front door, and Julie followed him into a high-ceilinged, oak-floored entrance hall. They walked through a huge dining room filled with antique furniture to the modern kitchen. Harvey padded into the room, looking sorrowful but wagging his tail. After greeting Brian with a low woof and a sloppy dog kiss, he turned his attention to Julie.

"Hey, I think he remembers me," Julie said, laughing as she scratched his floppy ears.

"He's not as dumb as he looks," Brian said. "But he's got to go out now. Come on, Harvey." The basset hound waddled out the door, looking at Brian reproachfully. "He'd rather lie on the living room rug, but he needs the exercise," Brian told Julie. "If the weather is nice, we make him stay out most of the day."

"Want something to drink?" Brian asked after they took off their coats.

When Julie nodded, Brian got two sodas out of the refrigerator and grabbed a bag of potato chips from a cupboard. "This should hold us over for a while."

"Where are your brothers?" Julie asked as they sat down at the kitchen table.

"Kevin's at swim practice, and Tom has a piano lesson. Speaking of them, we'd better get busy. Once they come home, it'll be a madhouse."

"Okay." Julie took a sip of her soda to ease the sudden dryness in her throat.

"So, what exactly did you have in mind?" Brian asked.

"Actually, I have several ideas," Julie said. "I thought I'd see which you liked best."

Brian nodded. "Great."

"Let me get my notes." Julie dug her lists out of her book bag. Rather than handing them over to him at once, she decided to talk about her ideas first. Then if Brian rejected them, he wouldn't know how much work she had put into her outlines.

Taking a deep breath, she started with her favorite idea—the one she had come up with the first time she and Trisha talked about the column. "I was thinking of comparing our dress code with Washington High's. I don't think Washington's dress code is nearly as strict as ours. I could get copies of the dress codes and compare them, then interview some kids from both schools. If the results are what I suspect, I'd argue that different dress codes in the same school district are unfair."

"That's not a bad idea, but I don't know about using it for your next column." Brian frowned. "It's going to take a lot of research."

"I could handle it," Julie insisted.

"Of course you could, but not in time for the next issue. Why don't you start working on that one for a few weeks from now?"

Julie controlled the urge to argue. After all, he hadn't rejected her idea outright. And she had two more. "All right," she said, and turned to her next sheet. "What about an article on the open/closed campus issue?"

But before she could explain how she planned to develop her topic, Brian shook his head. "We printed a column on that last year."

"I don't remember it," Julie said, frowning.

"That's because you didn't read the opinion column."

"I could read it now, then take another angle," Julie suggested.

Brian shook his head again. "No. Even if you take a completely different approach, people will say you stole the idea. Maybe next year."

Julie was beginning to feel a little desperate by now. She only had one more idea. What if he hated that one, too? She picked up a handful of chips and munched on them, stalling for time.

"What else do you have?" Brian asked.

Well, here goes, Julie thought. "How about a column on how kids really feel about their parents? We're always griping about them, but do we mean it? I'd identify the issues that really bother kids, as opposed to the things they just like to complain about. I could interview some students, talk to a few parents—"

"I don't think so," Brian said, cutting her off.

"Why not?" Julie asked angrily.

Brian shrugged. "It's boring. That's what made people stop reading the opinion column in the first place, remember?"

"Maybe it's boring to *you*, but it isn't to me, and I bet a lot of other kids at Memorial feel the same way!" Julie shouted. "Anyway, I don't have any more ideas!"

"Just calm down, Julie." Brian reached for her hand, but she snatched it away. "I'm sure we can think of something if we put our heads together."

"*We?* This is supposed to be *my* column, not yours!"

"Julie, will you stop yelling? I'm just trying to help."

"I'm not yelling," she yelled. "Since you know so much about everything, why don't you just write the stupid column yourself?" She jumped up, grabbed her coat and book bag, then raced out of the room, muttering, "I resign!"

Brian rose and followed her to the front door. "Where are you going?"

"Home!"

"At least let me give you a ride," he offered.

"No way!" she snapped as she flung the door open and ran out.

"But, Julie . . ." Brian called after her.

She ignored him and kept walking. After almost a block, she decided to peek back toward his house. The front door was shut, and the sidewalk was empty.

Great. Just great, she thought miserably. It was at least two miles to her house, and she wasn't wearing her walking shoes. As if that wasn't bad enough, her quick temper had cost her the job on the paper and her boyfriend. What else could possibly go wrong?

She had another mile and a half to go when it began to rain.

Chapter Ten

The drizzle soon turned into a storm. By the time Julie got home, she was soaked to the skin. Even her books and papers were soggy. She couldn't believe that Brian hadn't come after her in the car. Even though she'd said she didn't want a ride, it hadn't been raining then. If he cared about her at all, he wouldn't have let her almost drown!

Over the next three days, Brian approached her in the halls at school several times and called every night, but Julie refused to speak to him. Nothing he could say would make things right between them again.

On Friday afternoon, Julie went home with Trisha, hoping to forget about the long, lonely weekend that stretched ahead. They had just settled themselves in Trisha's room with assorted snacks from her secret supply when the phone on Trisha's bedside table rang. Trisha answered, and Julie heard her say, "Oh, hi—uh—yes, she is, as a matter of fact . . ." Covering the mouthpiece with her hand, Trisha whispered urgently, "Julie, it's Brian. He says it's important."

"Why did you tell him I was here?" Julie asked unnerved. "You know I don't want to talk to him!"

"I'm sorry. I just wasn't thinking. But it's too late now. What should I tell him?"

Julie scowled. "Tell him to take a long walk off a short pier!"

"I can't do that." Trisha was shocked. "It's rude."

"Brian Frederickson won't mind," Julie snapped. "He wrote the book on rude! Just tell him I'm busy, okay?" Julie persisted.

"She says she's busy," Trisha said into the receiver. ". . . No, I don't think that would be a good idea . . . I know, but there's nothing I can do. You know how she can be."

Julie resented the way they were talking about her, but just because she was mad at Brian, she could hardly forbid Trisha to talk to him.

"I don't know," Trisha said. "Well, I'll try. "Bye." She hung up the phone.

"What did he say?" Julie demanded.

"What do you care? You don't like him any- more, right?"

"Come on, Trisha," Julie said. "You're sup- posed to be my friend."

"Oh, all right." Trisha said and sighed dra- matically. "It's no big secret. He wants me to get you to see him, and I said I'd try."

Julie shook her head. "No way! Nothing I ever do or say is good enough for Mr. Know-It- All Frederickson. He doesn't like any of my ideas, and he hates the way I write. My feel- ings don't matter to him at all."

"He says he misses you," Trisha said softly. "Maybe you should talk to him, Julie. You told me he's called every day this past week."

"I don't care if he calls every day for a *year*! I have my pride." Julie wiped away a tear that trickled down her cheek. "Now let's see if we can figure out this geometry assignment. We don't want to spend the rest of the afternoon doing homework."

"How about a game of checkers?" Mr. Davis asked that evening after supper.

"I'm not really in the mood, Dad. Sorry."

Her father shook his head. "That's hard to believe, especially since you usually beat me. Do you feel okay?"

"I guess so." Julie said indifferently and glanced at the television screen without interest. "I just don't feel like doing anything right now."

"That's too bad. With your mother at that social work convention, I thought we'd have a chance to do something together, just the two of us."

"I'm really sorry, Dad." Julie let out another heavy sigh.

"Do you want to tell me about whatever's bothering you?"

Julie smiled weakly. "Is it that obvious?"

Mr. Davis nodded. "You might as well be wearing an 'I am miserable' button. Come on, honey. What's up? Have you and Brian had a fight?"

"Yes," Julie admitted.

"You want to tell me about it?" her father coaxed, sitting down next to her on the couch.

Prompted by an occasional question, Julie told him the whole story. She finished by saying, "I don't want to talk to him, but do you think I should give him a chance to apologize?"

Her father looked troubled. "Julie, I hate to ask you this, but are you sure this is all Brian's fault?"

"He rejects every idea I have, ruins my work behind my back, makes me walk home in the rain, and you think it's *my* fault?" she asked incredulously.

"I didn't say that," Mr. Davis replied. "But it takes two to argue, you know."

"I can't *believe* this!" Julie exclaimed. "You always tell me to stand up for myself, and now you want me to let some stupid boy walk all over me? Well, I won't stand for it!"

"All I'm saying is that I think you should hear Brian's side of the story," Mr. Davis said quietly.

"After he left me out in the rain? I almost drowned!" Julie glared at her father. "I should have known you'd defend him. You men always stick together!"

"Julie, that's ridiculous," her father said, exasperated. "I'm just concerned because you're so unhappy, and I'm suggesting that maybe you ought to try to see the situation from Brian's point of view, that's all." Then he smiled at her. "What about that game of checkers now? It might take your mind off your troubles."

Deep down, Julie knew her father was trying to help. She even suspected that she was being unreasonable, but she couldn't seem to help it.

"I'm kind of tired," she said stiffly. "I think I'll go to bed."

She could feel her father's worried eyes on her back as she walked out of the living room. By the time she got to her bedroom, she felt awful about the way she'd treated him. She knew she should go back downstairs and apologize, but not right now. She was just too miserable. She flipped off the bedside light, buried her face in her pillow, and cried herself to sleep.

"Whose idea was this, anyway?" Lisa asked, laughing hysterically the next morning.

"Yours," Julie said. "You told me that tennis was easy to learn."

"So I was wrong." The girls picked up their scattered balls and collapsed on a park bench beside the public tennis court. They were both perspiring, even though the autumn air was very cool. Chasing tennis balls all over the place was hard work, Julie had discovered, but it kept her from thinking about Brian, and about how rude she had been to her father last night.

She'd been so embarrassed about her behavior that she'd pretended to sleep until Mr. Davis left for the airport to pick up her mother. She really wanted to apologize, but she decided to wait until later that day.

"Why don't we go back to my house for lunch?" Julie suggested. "I don't know about you, but I've had it with tennis for now, and it's almost noon."

"Sounds great, but I hope your house isn't too far away. I'm pooped!" Lisa fanned herself with the racket, then made a face. "Hey, this thing is full of holes!"

"Maybe that's why we couldn't hit anything," Julie said with a giggle. It felt so good to laugh. She hadn't had anything to laugh about for a long time.

The house was empty when Julie and Lisa got there, but Julie found sandwich meat and potato salad from the deli in the refrigerator, and a plate of homemade peanut butter cookies on the kitchen table.

Apparently her parents had stopped by the house before checking out some yard sales, instead of leaving straight from the airport as they had originally planned.

Julie poured two glasses of orange juice, and then Lisa helped her make some sandwiches.

They ate their lunch at the kitchen table, and when they were finished, Lisa cleared her throat.

"Julie, I feel kind of funny about asking you this, but I was hoping you could do me a favor."

"Sure, Lisa. What is it?"

"Remember when we were talking about Brian editing our work?"

Julie nodded. How could she forget?

"Well, like I said, I haven't had many problems so far, but my latest article is making me crazy. There's something wrong with it, but I can't figure out what. If I turn it in like this, I just know Brian will tear it apart."

Julie hadn't told Lisa that she had quit the

paper, and she decided that there was no point in mentioning it now. "How can I help?" she asked instead.

"Would you read it and give me your opinion, even help me fix it?"

"I don't know, Lisa," Julie hedged. "What if I just make it worse?"

"Trust me, you *can't* make it any worse," Lisa insisted. "I have it in my purse. Please take a look, Julie."

"Okay," Julie said reluctantly. Who was she to edit anyone else's work since Brian hated everything she wrote? "I can't promise I'll be much help, though."

"Any help is better than none." Lisa rummaged through her purse and pulled out two sheets of paper.

Julie took them and began to read. *MEMORIAL HIGH WELCOMES NEW SECRETARY* was the headline. The article went on to give the secretary's name and work background, her husband's name and occupation, and her children's names and hobbies. Julie stared at the paper. Talk about boring . . .!

What could she possibly say? The article had practically put her to sleep. Lisa had said she wanted the truth, but Julie doubted if she wanted *that* much truth.

"Well, what do you think?" Lisa asked eagerly.

"Uh . . ." Julie took a deep breath. "Well, it reads sort of like—an obituary."

"An *obituary*?" Lisa echoed, dismayed.

"Well, it's kind of flat. There's no color to it."

"But it's *news*, not fiction," Lisa protested. "It's not my fault Mrs. Banes has led such a boring life!"

"I'm not suggesting that you add stuff that isn't true," Julie said. "That's not what I meant."

"Well, what *did* you mean?"

"Maybe you could reword it a little. For instance, here where you say, 'Mrs. Banes is originally from Memphis, Tennessee,' you could say 'A true daughter of the Confederacy, Mrs. Banes hails from Memphis, Tennessee.' Or, 'Mrs. Banes is a true Southern belle. She lived in Memphis before coming to Davenport.' It's kind of corny, but at least it's lively. You could probably come up with something much better."

"I don't know," Lisa said doubtfully. "Won't it sound like I just stuck that stuff in to make the piece longer?"

"No," Julie said, feeling some of her confidence returning. "It will help your readers become interested in the facts you're reporting, even if the facts aren't all that interesting on their own." As she talked, her confidence grew. "Here's another example. Instead of saying her hobbies are racquetball and scuba diving, you could say 'the fast pace of racquetball, which Mrs. Banes enjoys, pre-

116

pares her for our busy school office.' Or you might compare her scuba diving to digging through old files in the basement."

"But reporters are supposed to be concise. They're just supposed to tell who, what, when, where, and how," Lisa said stubbornly, frowning.

"They're also supposed to keep people interested so they'll keep reading," Julie pointed out, "not put them to sleep." The words slipped out before she could stop them.

"Oh, thanks!" Lisa snapped. "So you think my article will put my readers to sleep!" She looked as if she were about to burst into tears.

"That's not what I meant," Julie said again. "I mean, I guess it is what I *meant*, but I shouldn't have phrased it that way. I was just trying to help," she added lamely.

"Don't you like *anything* about my article?"

Julie scanned the pages a second time, searching desperately for some positive comment to make. "Well, it's very neatly typed, and you spelled all the words right," she said at last.

Now Lisa *did* burst into tears. "I'll never be a journalist," she cried. "I might as well just give up!"

Julie knew exactly how Lisa felt because she had felt the same way when Brian had criticized her work. How could she have been so thoughtless?

"Please don't cry, Lisa," she said, handing her friend a napkin to use as a tissue. "I'm really sorry I hurt your feelings. Anyway, what do I know? Brian rewrites everything I do, and he doesn't even like any of the topics I suggest for my column—my *former* column, that is."

"What do you mean?" Lisa asked, sniffling.

"This week after Brian rejected three of my ideas in a row, I quit the *Gazette*."

Lisa gasped. "You're kidding! But I thought the two of you . . ."

"Not anymore," Julie said firmly. "Look, do you mind if we don't talk about it? To get back to your article, don't pay any attention to what I said. Brian might like it just the way it is."

"I doubt it," Lisa said with a grimace. "*I* don't even like it much. But I guess I was hoping you'd tell me I was wrong, and that it's wonderful. I'm going to take your advice and see if I can liven it up a little. Thanks for being honest with me, Julie."

Julie smiled. "Sorry I wasn't more tactful about it, but you're welcome. If Brian doesn't like the changes you make in your article, you can blame it on me."

Chapter Eleven

After Lisa left, Julie went back over their conversation about Lisa's article. How could she have made that comment about putting people to sleep? She'd been trying to be helpful, yet she'd said all the wrong things and she'd actually made her friend cry.

Was that what had happened when Brian talked to her about her work? Had he been trying to be helpful, too? She remembered their first argument. He'd started telling her that the piece was 'a little one-sided.' It was only when she flew off the handle that he had accused her of name-calling.

Brian had been wrong about what he'd allowed Tim to do to her column on the girls' athletic program, there was no question in Julie's mind about that. But he had admitted it, once she'd given him the chance. He'd even apologized, and promised not to do it again. Now that Julie really thought about it, their fight about the subject for her next column hadn't been all Brian's fault. He hadn't completely rejected all her ideas. In fact he'd approved one of them for a future issue.

But she hadn't been as reasonable as Lisa was this afternoon. Lisa had been upset, too, but she hadn't run off, cutting their discussion short before Julie had a chance to explain. If Julie had stayed and talked to Brian, they might have worked out some kind of compromise.

Then Julie frowned. Even if she was willing to admit she was partly to blame for their last argument, what about the way Brian had let her walk home in the pouring rain? What kind of a way was that to treat somebody you cared about? Yet, he had kept phoning her, and he'd told Trisha he missed her. . . .

But he hadn't called her today. Maybe he'd finally decided that he didn't care about her after all. Julie sighed. Well, she'd blown it for sure. She'd know better next time. If she had to work with someone on a project, she would try very hard not to let her feelings be hurt if they disagreed with her, and she'd try even harder to control her temper. She'd also think twice before dating a boy she was working with.

There was no use worrying about it any longer, though. Now it was time to get on with her life as best as she could. Julie went into the bathroom and got the home permanent she'd bought last month. Until now, she hadn't had the nerve to try it, but maybe a new hairstyle would make her feel less depressed. The curly-haired model on the box certainly seemed happy enough.

Several hours later, Julie's hair was dry and *very* curly, and the mess was all cleaned up. She heard the back door open, and the sound of her parents' voices. Julie glanced in the mirror one last time before she went downstairs. The mass of curls framing her face was very becoming, she decided, wondering how her mother and father would react.

"Be careful when you come around that doorway, Allan," Mrs. Davis was saying as Julie came into the kitchen.

"Hi, Mom. How was your trip?" she called out.

"Good, honey. Thanks."

Julie watched as her mother backed in through the outside door, holding one end of an odd-looking oak and brass contraption. A moment later, her father appeared, holding the other end.

"What *is* that thing?" Julie asked.

"It's a coat tree," her mother answered as she and Julie's father set it down.

"Doesn't look like a tree to me," Julie said, giggling.

Mr. Davis glanced at her and blinked in exaggerated surprise. "Will you look at that, Carol? Somebody stole our daughter away while we were gone. See what they left in her place!"

"What are you talking about?" Mrs. Davis questioned as she turned to hug Julie hello. "Oh, my! You curled your hair!" she gasped.

"Don't you like it?" Julie bit her lower lip. What if her perm wasn't becoming after all? What if it really looked awful? She would be stuck with it for months.

"Of course we like it, Julie," her mother said, smiling. "You just surprised us."

"Good, because it's a perm. I did it myself," Julie added proudly.

Her father smiled, too. "Your hair looks beautiful, sweetheart. *All* of you looks beautiful."

"Well, I think this calls for a celebration," Mrs. Davis said. "Julie has a new hairstyle, and we have the coat tree we've been wanting for ages. Suppose I make a reservation for dinner at that new Italian restaurant? Do you two think you can handle that?"

They both agreed enthusiastically. As Mrs. Davis walked out of the kitchen, Julie glanced

122

over at her father. He seemed to have forgotten all about last night's argument, but Julie hadn't.

"Dad, about last night . . ." She wasn't quite sure where to go from there.

"Yes, honey?"

"I wasn't very nice." She took a deep breath. "Some of the things I said were unfair, and I'm sorry. I was just so upset that I felt like the whole world was against me."

"I know how that can be." Mr. Davis put his arm around her and gave her a hug. "Sometimes things make us angry because we're afraid there's some truth in them."

"So you're telling me that I got mad at you because I realized that the mess with Brian was partly my fault?"

"Something like that. Are you going to get mad at me again?" he asked, smiling.

"No." Julie grinned sheepishly. "I gave the whole thing a lot of thought today. I know I could have handled it a lot better. And my friend Lisa taught me something, too." She told him about how she'd tried to help Lisa with her article, and had only made her cry. "Maybe Brian didn't mean to hurt my feelings, either."

Her father nodded. "It's a definite possibility. So what are you going to do?"

"There's nothing I *can* do about Brian," she said sadly. "Besides, I'm still mad at him for leaving me stranded in the rain. Maybe I'll try to get my job back on the paper one of these days, though. And the next time I like a boy— if there *is* a next time—I'll be a lot smarter about it!"

Chapter Twelve

On Sunday afternoon Julie was wandering from room to room, trying to decide what to do. Her parents had gone to visit some relatives, and she had opted to stay home. A quick flip through the channels convinced her there was nothing interesting on TV, and she didn't feel like reading.

Julie went to her room and dug her poetry notebook out of a drawer. She sat down and picked up a pen and waited, but inspiration didn't strike. Finally, she tossed her notebook onto the bed and headed back downstairs to the kitchen. Maybe she should try baking something. Those cookies she'd made for the picnic with Brian had been a big hit.

Thinking about what a good time they'd had together that day made her feel sad for a minute. That was the day he'd asked her to go skiing. It would never happen now.

Julie tried to thrust the depressing thought away and tied an apron around her waist. No use moping. Maybe when the cookies were made, she would call Trisha and Lisa and ask them to come over and have some.

Following the recipe wasn't nearly as hard as it had been the first time, and Julie soon finished making the dough. She was just putting the last batch into the oven when the doorbell rang. Grabbing a paper towel, she wiped the flour and shortening off her fingers and ran to answer it.

Julie's jaw dropped when she opened the front door and saw Brian standing there. He was wearing a bulky ski sweater, and one hand clutched a bunch of slightly drooping daisies.

"Julie, please don't slam the door," he said softly. "These are for you." He held the daisies out in front of him.

Julie didn't know what to do or say. Should she take the flowers, or slam the door in his face? No, she couldn't shut him out, especially since she realized their fights had been partly her fault. Besides, he looked so cute standing there, a hopeful half-smile curving the corners of his mouth. "Thank you," she murmured, taking the flowers.

"I know they're a little wilted. . . ." Brian said.

"That's okay," she said quickly. Now what should she do? All this indecision was making her heart pound. But she couldn't just keep standing there staring at him like an idiot, so she asked, "Do you want to come in for a minute?"

"Sure." He stepped into the hall. "You changed your hair. It looks cute like that."

"Thanks," Julie started to smile at the compliment, but the smile soon faded. How would her new curls have looked after the drenching she'd gotten last Tuesday? There was another long, awkward silence. This time Brian broke it.

"I guess you're wondering why I'm here." He suddenly seemed pretty nervous.

"You're right," Julie said.

"I tried to talk to you, but you wouldn't take my calls."

She shrugged. "I didn't think we had anything to say to each other." She almost added a few remarks about what kind of person would let another person walk home in a rainstorm, but she caught herself. If she was even considering asking for her job back on the paper, she'd better not pick another fight.

"Julie, I have plenty to say," Brian said. "I was trying to apologize. That's why I came here today. I felt terrible about the other day,

127

especially when it started raining. You must have gotten soaked."

"So kind of you to notice," she said sarcastically. "Too bad you didn't notice in time to give me a lift."

Brian sighed. "I don't blame you for being mad. You must have thought I was a real jerk, letting you walk home in the rain."

"That's about the size of it," she agreed. "I figured *you* figured it would serve me right if I drowned!"

"Julie, I didn't!" he exclaimed, exasperated. "I wanted to pick you up, but the car wouldn't start. I guess the battery was almost dead, and I ran it down the rest of the way trying to get it going. I had to buy a new battery, and spark plugs, too."

The tight knot in Julie's stomach began to unwind. "I thought you just didn't care," she said softly.

"You would have had a right to be mad even if that hadn't happened," Brian said. "I admit, I was pretty rude about your ideas. In fact . . ." He wrinkled his nose. "What's that smell?"

"Smell?" Julie sniffed, then shrieked, "Oh, no! My cookies!"

As she dashed for the kitchen, she heard Brian's footsteps following her. "Can I help?" he asked.

"It's too late." Julie grimaced as she pulled her baking sheet out of the oven. The cookies were coal-black. "Too bad you didn't bring Harvey. He probably loves burned cookies."

Brian laughed. He grabbed a spatula and scooped up one of the cookies, blowing on it to cool it. Then he bit into it. "They're—not *that* bad," he said, making a face.

Julie picked one up and took a bite. "You're right. They're not bad, they're *awful,*" she exclaimed. "They're not even fit for Harvey!"

"Sure they are. Charcoal's good for dogs," Brian said with a grin.

"If you say so. You can take this batch home to him."

Julie slid the burned cookies into a plastic bag, then put the blackened cookie sheet in the sink to soak. She stole a glance at Brian, wondering, *What now?* Was he going to finish what he had started to say a few minutes ago?

"Would you like a *good* cookie?" she asked when he didn't speak up immediately.

"You bet." Brian picked one of the unburned ones and bit into it. This time he smiled as he chewed. "These are even better than the ones you baked for our picnic." When he had finished the cookie, he said, "I was hoping maybe we could talk and straighten things out between us. I'm really sorry for the things I said."

Julie's heart leapt with joy. "I'm sorry, too," she said. "I guess I kind of overreacted. What you said wasn't so awful."

"Well, I could have said it better."

"True," Julie said. She piled some cookies on a plate and poured two glasses of milk. "Why don't we take these into the living room and talk while we eat?"

"Great. Here, let me help." Brian picked up the glasses and followed her.

Julie sat at one end of the sofa and set the plate of cookies on the coffee table. Brian sat down next to her and when he handed her glass to her, their fingers brushed, giving Julie a little thrill of excitement. Brian was so special. When they weren't fighting, he was the sweetest boy she'd ever met. If only they could work things out between them!

"After you left, I thought about the way we've been fighting over your column," Brian said. "I realized that some of the things I said came out sounding pretty terrible. I didn't mean them that way, Julie, and I had no idea you'd get so upset."

"Why shouldn't I be upset when you say my topics are boring and trite? Or when you accuse me of slandering people? Should I just smile and say 'Yes sir, I'll do it your way'?" As she recalled what he had said about her last three ideas, Julie felt her temper begin to rise, but she controlled it. Instead of blowing up, this time she would listen to what he had to say.

Brian pushed a lock of hair out of his eyes.

"Of course not. I'd argue, too. But we never seem to get past the arguing stage, so we don't find a way to compromise."

"How can we compromise when you say 'do it my way or else'?" Julie asked, frowning.

"Do I really do that?" Brian looked surprised.

"Always. The first time, you said you wouldn't print my column unless I revised it the way you wanted it. The next time, you told Tim to change it without even consulting me. I've tried to be cooperative, Brian, I really have, but then when you shot down three of my ideas in a row, it was just too much!"

Brian shook his head slowly. "Was I really that bad? My folks are always telling me I'm stubborn, but I never believed them. I spend half my life arguing with my brothers. As soon as they learned to talk, I found that the only way to hold my own was to act as if I was always right. Now, whenever there's a disagreement, I guess I behave the same way. Maybe that's why you and I have so much trouble."

"You mean, you and your brothers just keep arguing until someone gives in?" Julie asked, astonished. She couldn't imagine it. "What if you hurt each other's feelings?"

"It isn't quite as bad as it sounds." Brian looked sheepish. "I mean, we don't beat each other up or anything. We don't really believe the angry things we say to each other, so our

131

feelings don't get hurt, and we always reach some kind of a compromise."

"In my family, if one of us has a problem, we discuss it until we reach a solution that satisfies everyone," Julie said.

"We get there, but there's usually a lot of yelling first," Brian said, grinning.

"We just don't do that. Mom and Dad hardly ever argue, and they almost never yell at me. Sometimes I raise my voice a little," she admitted, blushing as she remembered her argument with her father. "But I'm trying to learn not to. Anyway, what does this have to do with the fact that you hate my writing?"

"I *don't* hate your writing," Brian said. "In fact, I think you're one of my best writers. Just because I ask you to change some things doesn't mean I don't like the way you write. I ask the other reporters on the *Gazette* to change stuff, too."

"What if they don't want to?"

"We argue about it until we reach a compromise."

"So if I'd kept arguing with you that first time instead of walking out, you might have let me keep some of the things you objected to?" Julie asked. This was all pretty confusing, but she thought she was beginning to understand.

"Sure. I was amazed when you handed in your revised column, and you'd done everything I asked."

132

"*Ordered,* you mean," Julie corrected. "I didn't know I even had a choice." She thought for a minute. "So if I'd really pushed the idea of a column on dress codes, you might have let me do it."

"If you had convinced me you could've gotten it done," Brian admitted. "It really *is* too late for this issue now, though. The deadline's just five days away."

Julie suddenly realized that he must have forgotten she'd quit the paper. Or maybe he just hadn't heard her say she was resigning when she had dashed out the door. If Brian didn't even know she'd quit, she wouldn't have to ask for her job back.

"So, do you forgive me?" Brian asked anxiously. "And do you want to go to the movies this afternoon?"

"I suppose so." Then Julie added, "If we're going to start seeing each other again, I'd better make a confession. Every time you said something bad about my writing, I thought you were saying you didn't care about me anymore. That's another reason I got so upset."

"I'd care about you even if you couldn't spell cat," Brian said earnestly.

Julie smiled. "I'm glad. But from now on, I think we should try to keep our work on the *Gazette* separate from our personal lives."

"You mean, we shouldn't talk about the paper when we go out on a date?" Brian asked.

Julie nodded. "Also, we should stick to business when we *are* working on the paper."

"No stealing kisses, huh?" Brian teased. He moved over even closer to her. "You know what? We're not working now."

Julie's heart raced wildly as he put his arms around her and very gently kissed her on the lips.

When they finally came up for air, she said a little shakily, "Maybe we should talk about my next column. We can't just keep kissing until it's time for the movie!"

Brian grinned. "Why not?" Julie poked him and he released her, laughing. "Okay, okay. We'll get down to business. Do you want to skip this issue and do your dress code survey for the next one?"

"I'd like to do the dress code column for the next issue, but I just had a great idea for this one." Julie smiled mischievously. "It's a subject that will interest everyone. Maybe teachers, too."

"What is it? You only have five days, remember."

"This won't take long, and I've already done most of the research. I thought I'd write about male/female communication problems, and how to solve them."

Brian grinned. "Good idea. Just don't mention any names, okay?"

"Okay," Julie said, laughing.

"You know," Brian said, "my family is going fishing next weekend. Want to come? It'll probably be pretty chilly, but we'll build a campfire and stuff. It'll be fun."

"I'd love to," Julie said, glowing with happiness. "But I don't know how to fish."

"I'll show you what to do, and I'll even bait your hook," Brian offered, smiling. "Come on, you'll love it."

Julie shook her head, smiling. She was catching on. Brian always tried to get his way, but from now on, she wasn't always going to let him. "You fish. I'll read a book or something."

Brian shrugged. "Okay, have it your way. Hey, maybe we could try something new this winter."

"Such as?" Julie asked.

"I've always wanted to go snowshoeing," Brian said.

"That doesn't sound very exciting," Julie replied. "I'd rather go skiing, like you mentioned on our picnic."

"I don't know . . ." Brian thought for a moment. "I've got it! How about cross-country skiing?"

"Great idea," Julie said with a smile. Then she asked, "Do you realize what we just did?"

He looked confused. "We made a date."

"That's not all," Julie said. "We talked until we found something we both wanted to do, and then we compromised."

135

"You're right!" Brian's grin widened. "It wasn't all that difficult, either!"

"Do you want some more cookies?" she asked, noticing that the cookie plate was empty.

"A couple more couldn't hurt," Brian admitted.

"I'll be right back." Julie picked up the plate and left the room.

In the hallway, she hesitated. She wanted to share something special with Brian, to prove how much she trusted him. But how far did her trust go? Could she trust him with her most intimate feelings?

Sometimes you have to take a chance, she decided, and hurried upstairs to her bedroom. It took only a few minutes to find the poem she wanted. Carefully, she tore it out of her notebook, folded it, and put it in her pocket.

After refilling the cookie plate, she walked back into the living room and sat down beside Brian.

"What took you so long?" he asked, slipping an arm around her. "I thought you got lost."

"I was looking for something." Julie looked down, suddenly shy.

"What?"

"Well . . ." She hesitated. "Once you said you'd like to see some of my poetry," she murmured, taking the piece of paper out of her pocket.

"I'd love to," Brian said softly. "May I read it?"

Julie let him take the paper, then held her breath. To her surprise, he began to read aloud.

"SPRING SONG

Roots pressing into soft, black earth,
Branches reaching for the sky,
New leaves rustling in the breeze,
Blossoms bursting.
Our friendship grows just like the tree,
Nourished by the trust we share,
Watered by our joy, to blossom into love."

"Julie, that's beautiful," he said. "Really beautiful. And it's really good, too. May I print it in the *Gazette*?"

Julie smiled. "Are you sure you don't want any changes?"

"Not a one," Brian said with a grin. "There *is* something I want, though."

"What's that?"

"This." He drew her close to him and kissed her, first playfully on the nose, then on the lips.

When they parted, Julie sighed with happiness as she rested her head against his shoulder. "You can do that any time you like," she said with a smile. "Except, of course, when we're working."

"So can you, Julie." Brian looked deeply into her eyes. "It's hard for me to always make the first move," he confessed.

Julie's heart opened to him. She realized that boys might hide it better, but they were sometimes just as nervous and unsure of themselves as girls were.

"Well, since we're both learning to compromise . . ." Smiling, she slipped her arms around his neck. "I suppose it wouldn't hurt me to kiss you, too."

And she did.

We hope you enjoyed reading this book. If you would like to receive further information about available titles in the Bantam series, just write to the address below, with your name and address: Kim Prior, Bantam Books, 61–63 Uxbridge Road, Ealing, London W5 5SA.

If you live in Australia or New Zealand and would like more information about the series, please write to:

Sally Porter
Transworld Publishers
(Australia) Pty Ltd
15–25 Helles Avenue
Moorebank
NSW 2170
AUSTRALIA

Kiri Martin
Transworld Publishers (NZ) Ltd
3 William Pickering Drive
Albany
Auckland
NEW ZEALAND

All Bantam and Young Adult books are available at your bookshop or newsagent, or can be ordered from the following address: Corgi/Bantam Books, Cash Sales Department, PO Box 11, Falmouth, Cornwall TR10 9EN.

Please list the title(s) you would like, and send together with a cheque or postal order to cover the cost of the book(s) plus postage and packing charges of £1.00 for one book, £1.50 for two books, and an additional 30p for each subsequent book ordered to a maximum of £3.00 for seven or more books.

(The above applies only to readers in the UK, and BFPO)

Overseas customers (including Eire), please allow £2.00 for postage and packing for the first book, an additional £1.00 for a second book, and 50p for each subsequent title ordered.